just

like

jackie

LINDSEY STODDARD

HARPER

An Imprint of HarperCollins Publishers

Just Like Jackie

Copyright © 2018 by Lindsey Stoddard

All rights reserved. Printed in the United States of America.

No part of this book may be used or reproduced in any manner whatsoever without

written permission except in the case of brief quotations embodied in critical articles

and reviews. For information address HarperCollins Children's Books, a division of

HarperCollins Publishers, 195 Broadway, New York, NY 10007.

www.harpercollinschildrens.com

Library of Congress Control Number: 2017942891

ISBN 978-0-06-265292-8

Typography by Sarah Nichole Kaufman

20 21 22   BRR   10 9 8 7 6 5

❖

First paperback edition, 2019

For
Nana and Pop
&
Grandma and Grandpa

Praise for *Just Like Jackie*:

★ "Stoddard debuts with a quiet but powerful narrative that gently unpacks Alzheimer's, centers mental health, and moves through the intimate and intense emotional landscape of family—what seems to break one and what can remake it. Validating, heart-rending, and a deft blend of suffering and inspiration."

—*Kirkus Reviews* (starred review)

★ "This emotionally honest, sensitively written novel confronts a range of difficult topics and offers an inclusive view of what family can look like."

—*Publishers Weekly* (starred review)

"I was truly moved by this refreshing story about a scrappy young heroine and her struggle to protect her family."

—Sara Pennypacker, *New York Times* bestselling author of *Pax*

"*Just Like Jackie* is not the story I thought it was going to be, and that's because it's a story about scratching the surface (and welcoming what you find below). It's also a lovely story of acceptance—about what makes a family and how we make our own families, and about embracing our differences."

—Ann M. Martin, *New York Times* bestselling author of *Rain Reign*

"As close to perfect as a book for middle-grade children can get! Readers will cheer for Robbie as she comes to terms with the family she has and finds the family she needs."

—Cammie McGovern, author of *Just My Luck*

"A fresh coming-of-age novel as feisty, funny, and forthright as its protagonist. Robinson overcomes obstacles with wit, grit, and a growing compassion for others. A rich, rewarding read all around."

—John David Anderson, author of *Ms. Bixby's Last Day*

"A home-run story that will resonate with all who feel they might not fit into the perfect definition of a family." —*School Library Journal*

"Debut author Stoddard crafts a winning narrator in Robinson. A beautiful story about the true meaning of family, perfect for fans of Lynda Mullaly Hunt."

—ALA *Booklist*

Also by Lindsey Stoddard
Right as Rain

chapter 1

Before I know it I have Alex Carter's nose blood on me. My fist is tingling and his blood is squirted up the right sleeve of my sweatshirt. Everyone is crowding around, and Alex is crying like some tiny baby.

"She's crazy!" he screams and points right at me. "She punched me!"

He shouldn't have called me Robin. Maybe his face would be all in one piece and he wouldn't be sobbing like a weenie if he knew when to shut his mouth.

Baseballs drop to the hard-packed snow and all the players rush to third base, where Alex is crying and I'm standing over him. Everyone else is abandoning their snowmen and games of tag and running fast to surround us. "Fight! Fight! Fight!"

They're probably all thinking it's about time Alex Carter got popped. And they're right.

Derek's fumbling over now too, as fast as he can, and yelling, "Robbie! Wait!" but his feet are too big and he's the slowest kid in the grade and he'd be no help in a fight anyway. Too scrawny.

The teachers are sprinting across the yard to get between us, but I'm in ready position. Right fist up to strike if I have to. Left hand inside my baseball glove, blocking my face. I should have known Alex wouldn't do anything but cry and bleed in the snow. He's the biggest bully in the fifth grade, but I shut him up good. He's not laughing at me now and flapping his arms and calling me a motherless Robin bird.

A splatter of red is drying on my sleeve, but I don't give a crap. Tough people look tough. That's why Alex has long flowy blond hair like feathers and baby-blanket-blue eyes. And why my knuckles have his blood on them.

And he was calling *me* a bird. I don't have any feathers, nothing soft like that. My hair is blond too. But *dirty* blond. Not all white and fluffy, and I don't wear it loose and flowy like he does. Mine is pulled back in two thick braids under my Dodgers hat. The braids aren't perfect either because Grandpa doesn't always pull them tight enough. So by the end of the day all my curls give up on being good and start popping out left and right. I know how that feels.

Alex is blubbering now, and spraying snotty blood from his nose like it's going to kill him. It splatters like spilled transmission fluid, red splotches across the white ground. Grandpa taught me how to seal transmission fluid leaks under the hood of a 1999 Honda Civic at the garage. But I'm happy to let Alex sop up his bloody nose with the sleeve of his sissy-boy snowboarding jacket. There's no sealing up a kid that's gone that bad. I should know.

"What's wrong with her?" he screams. White puffs of sad, sorry bully breath escape from his crying mouth.

The first teacher that gets there is telling him to tip his head back and pinch his nose and asking if he's all right and making a big deal.

Derek's still running and yelling, "It's not her fault!" which feels pretty OK because it's true and no one else will believe me. But Derek does.

Then Mr. Danny has me by the shoulders. "That was *not* very ladylike," he says all mean and close-jawed and under his breath like he's sick of me but also maybe secretly glad someone finally gave that pest Alex what he deserved.

"What kind of ladies are you talking about?" I say. "The prissy, snap-in-half kind who let stupid boys call them names?"

He pushes me away from Alex and toward the front door of the school, and all the kids who are out for recess are staring at me with their jaws hanging open.

Derek's following behind us now and he's out of breath. "Not . . . her . . . fault . . ." Mr. Danny shoos him off. "Let . . . her—"

But no one can hear the rest of what Derek is stammering because Alex Baby Carter yells out, "That's why people need moms! Or they'll end up like her!" He's crying at the same time, so he sounds all pathetic, but I'm not letting him get away with that crap.

I try to wiggle out of Mr. Danny's hold, but he tightens his grip on my shoulders. So I whip around and shout back, "You turned out mean and weak and pathetic! What does that say about your mom?"

"Robbie!" Derek exclaims and pumps his purple fleece mitten in the air. And I can't tell if he's cheering me on or trying to get me to shut my mouth so I don't get in any more trouble than I'm already in. But either way I know he's got my back.

The rest of the kids in the yard are still just standing around with their mouths hanging open. Mr. Danny nudges me across the yard toward the school.

No one talks about my mom. Not even Grandpa. Not ever.

I would listen to Grandpa if he talked about my mom,

and not get all mad. But he doesn't. Maybe because he forgets, the way he sometimes forgets why he folded his winter jacket and put it in his underwear drawer, or what goes first, socks or shoes. Or maybe he doesn't forget my mom at all. Maybe he just doesn't want to remember. I do, though. But I can't. Not without Grandpa. And every time I ask he closes up tighter than a rusted bolt.

The front door slams behind us as Mr.Danny walks me into Principal Wheeler's office. I pull away and slump in one of the office chairs. No other kids are here. No other kids are ever here because this is a school of chickens. I don't even know why they have so many chairs in the office. They just need one. Mine.

"You'll have to call Robinson's grandfather," he tells Ms. Burg, the office lady. She sighs like this is old news and picks up the phone. "This time we'll need him to come in."

"Come in?" I sit up fast. "My grandpa's not coming here. You can just suspend me and I'll walk to his garage and help him work on the cars."

Mr. Danny puts his hand on my shoulder and I shake it off. "That's not how it works, Robinson. What you did today is really serious."

Ms. Burg dials and holds the phone pinched between her ear and shoulder and I'm staring at the big clock on the wall above her head. It's afternoon already, which means Grandpa could be all turned around and confused, and if someone like a stupid office lady named Ms. Burg pulls him out of his routine it could be even worse.

"You don't have to call—"

"Enough, Robinson," she cuts.

"While you're at it, you better call Alex Carter's mom too," I say. "Because he's blubbering real hard out there. I'm pretty sure I heard him cry for his mommy."

"Robinson." Ms. Burg looks at me over the tops of the green frames of her glasses and shakes her head. And I'm wondering if she got named Ms. Burg on purpose because it sounds like *bug* and she looks exactly like one with those dumb green glasses. Plus all she does is bug kids all day.

Then my grandpa must pick up the phone because she puts on her fake nice voice and chimes, "Yes. Is this Mr. Hart? This is Ms. Burg from Robinson's school. She's fine, she's sitting right here with me, but we'll need you to come down to the office. There's been a little incident." Then she swivels in her chair so I can't hear the rest.

Mr. Danny sits down in one of the bad-kid chairs next to me and looks right in my eyes. "Why did you do that?" he asks. "I just don't understand."

"I told you. He wouldn't stop calling me a little Robin bird, flapping his arms and acting like he's all funny. I warned him to stop." I look down at the blood drying on my fist, then punch it twice hard into the worn leather pocket of my baseball glove.

Mr. Danny doesn't say anything else, just blows a gust of disappointed air out of his nose.

"No one calls me Robin," I remind him. "How many times do I have to tell him that before it gets through his thick skull? My name's Robinson and I'm sick of his crap."

Mr. Danny shakes his head like I'm a lost cause and I'm good with that. Lost causes get suspended and work in their grandpas' garages for the rest of their lives and that is A-OK with me. Plus the ground is thawing and the sap is running and Grandpa could use my help collecting it from the maple trees we tapped, then boiling it into syrup. School just gets in the way of the stuff worth doing.

"Her grandpa is walking over now," Ms. Burg reports, pushing her glasses back up her nose and dialing another number.

"Hi, Mrs. Carter?" she chirps. "So sorry to have to bother you. I know this is a tough time—" She swivels her chair again so I can't hear the rest, but I bet it's all full of sugar because nothing Alex does is ever wrong and it's always my fault.

Then Alex Baby Carter comes in the office and they

sit him in a chair way on the other side, far from me. Good idea. He's holding a big wad of white gauze over his nose, the kind Grandpa and I have in our first-aid kit at home.

Ms. Burg tells him that his mom is on her way. "She's going to take you right to the doctor to get that nose checked out." He nods. Then she pokes her head into Principal Wheeler's private office. "Mr. Hart is on his way."

"Nobody calls me Robin," I tell Alex, slamming my fist harder into the pocket of my glove and staring right at him. Now I'm mad because it's Alex's fault that Grandpa has to walk over here by himself and it'll be his fault if Grandpa takes a wrong turn and ends up searching the shelves for something he can't remember at Dean and Walt's country store.

Alex sniffles and winces when he takes his hands off his nose. The blood's all dried up. "What kind of girl only wants to be called Robinson, Robbie, or Son?" he asks.

"The kind that just pounded your face."

"Robinson, that's enough," Mr. Danny cuts in.

It better be enough. Enough to shut Alex up for good.

The office door swings open and Grandpa hobbles in. His legs are shaped like he's been riding a horse all his life instead of fixing up cars and tapping maple trees. He moves more side to side than forward. His navy jumpsuit from the garage has his name, Charlie, stitched over his heart, and I wonder where his jacket is. It's cold out.

He takes one look at Alex's gigantic wad of blood-soaked gauze and says, "What in God's name . . ." with a voice that's as deep as the lines that run across his dark forehead. I shoot a glare at Alex that says, *You better not say a thing about how he can't be my real grandpa, or how I bet I wish my mom wasn't dead. Or else.*

Grandpa takes a long look at me, then down at the blood squirted up my sleeve, and he shakes his head. I hate making Grandpa shake his head.

"Mr. Hart, the principal is waiting to speak with you," Ms. Burg says, and she gestures toward the door that says *Principal Wheeler.*

I stand up to walk in with him, but Mr. Danny stops me. "This meeting is just for adults, Robinson." Then before I know it Ms. Gloria is there too and Mr. Danny is opening Principal Wheeler's door and telling me to sit back down.

"Shouldn't I be—"

But the door is closed and my grandpa is gone, into the principal's office like he did something bad and not me. And he doesn't even like to talk too much unless he's under the hood of a car, or splitting wood for the pile, and all these adults talking about their stupid school stuff will make him confused, and he didn't do anything wrong except get given a bad kid.

I almost wish I could take it back. Pull my fist out of Alex Carter's face and count to ten instead, like Ms. Gloria taught me. Count to ten, take three deep breaths, or repeat baseball stats until that's all I could think about—*Career leaders. Batting average: Ty Cobb, .366. Hits: Pete Rose, 4,256*—until I got calm again. Then maybe Grandpa wouldn't have to shake his head and go to the principal's office, and I wouldn't be such a pain in the butt, like a trailer that's too heavy for his small frame to tow.

chapter 2

When Principal Wheeler's office door opens and they all come out, the grooves on Grandpa's forehead look deeper.

Ms. Gloria sits down next to me and says, "We all agree that you need to go home with your grandpa today. Tomorrow we'll discuss some next steps about a behavior plan that will help you manage your anger in school."

"Tomorrow?" I shoot up from my seat. "I'm not suspended? What kind of school is this?"

"Robinson . . ." Ms. Gloria's got that voice she uses when she's trying to calm me down, soft and low and serious. But I don't care.

"Isn't it illegal in this state to punch someone in the face? Didn't I break a Vermont law? What kind of message are you sending, letting me stay here?"

Grandpa puts his hand on my shoulder and pats it three slow times. "You're lucky now, Robbie," he says with that deep voice all full of gravel and split wood. "You'll come with me today to cool off and get your head straight, because this is unacceptable."

Grandpa thanks Mr. Danny and Ms. Gloria. And then, as if things could get any worse, Alex's blond, flowy-haired mom shows up in black stockings and clicky high heels and a long black coat with big buttons. She looks like one of those prissy, snap-in-half-type ladies, but she has the same deep forehead lines that Grandpa does. I didn't realize people as young as regular mom and dad age could get those.

"I'm sure you'd like to apologize before you go," Mr. Danny says.

"No way—" I start, but Grandpa squeezes my shoulder hard like he's tightening lug nuts.

"Sorry." But I say it more to my untied Nike Air Griffeys than to Alex. "If you don't call me Robin anymore, I won't punch your face again." I cross my fingers behind my back just in case.

Grandpa tightens the lug nuts on my shoulder. "Try again."

This time I just mumble, "I'm sorry for what I did." But my fingers are still crossed.

Mrs. Carter looks up from her sniffling sissy Alex

and studies Grandpa's hand on my shoulder for a quick second that she thinks no one notices. "You're Robinson's . . ."

"Grandpa," I say. But I know what she's thinking. That we don't match. That Grandpa is the dark color of a motor oil leak and I'm light as power steering fluid on my darkest summer day. But it's none of her business.

"That's . . . very nice." But she raises her eyebrows when she says it, like grown-ups do when they're on to something, and it makes me wonder if she can see into Grandpa's tired memory and if she knows that sometimes he leaves his keys in the refrigerator and the milk by the door. Because that's nobody's business except Grandpa's and mine. But her raised eyebrows and long look make me feel hot and nervous, like we've got to get out of here fast because if someone finds out, they'll make it a huge deal like grown-ups always do. Then what?

Mrs. Carter looks straight down at me. "Keep your hands off my son." And when she's walking away with her arm around Alex, I hear her mumble "old man unfit to raise," but I can't catch the rest. And even though it makes my fists clench tight and I think that she deserves a nose to match her son's, before I know it I'm pulling Grandpa out the office door and away before he can mix up his words and anyone else raises their eyebrows and sees into our secret.

On the walk to the garage I stay one half step ahead of Grandpa so he just has to follow along in case his memory gets tired. I do that to him sometimes, make his memory tired. Whenever I'm bad he forgets more. That's why I have to try to be better.

"You can't be using your fists, Robbie," he tells me. "You're better than that."

"Alex deserved it," I say, because he did. "And not just for calling me a Robin bird. He's mean to everyone all the time behind teachers' backs, then acts all innocent when they're looking again."

"That doesn't make it right. Violence will get you . . ." But he's drifting off. And I know he means that violence will get me nowhere fast but he forgot the end of his sentence. And he's shaking his head again. I hate that so much.

I wait for Grandpa to tell me about Jackie Robinson like he always does when I do something bad. But he just goes along, saying nothing, and it doesn't feel right all quiet like that, so I tell it to myself in my head:

The man you're named for was a great ballplayer. The first black player in the league. People taunted him all the time, but he didn't pay no mind. He couldn't. Even if they called him names, he just let it roll right off. He had to.

And that's how I know I'm not much like the real Robinson. But Grandpa wishes I was.

He tells me about Jackie Robinson because he wants me to realize I have to do better. And that even when people are rotten, I shouldn't fight back.

But he's not even telling me today. He's just walking quiet, side to side, side to side, on his bowed legs. Maybe he doesn't know what to do with me anymore and he's giving up. Or maybe he's forgetting about Jackie Robinson too.

I want Grandpa to tell me about when he was five years old:

It was the first World Series televised in color and Jackie Robinson and the Dodgers beat the Yankees in seven games. The only World Series they won in Brooklyn.

But we just keep making small steps down the sidewalk.

Grandpa's hand is swinging there beside me, and I kind of catch it for a second in the pocket of my baseball glove and squeeze. He looks down like he's surprised I'm there, like he'd forgotten.

"I'll be more like Jackie Robinson, Grandpa."

He smiles at me and we walk on to the garage through the new falling snow.

chapter 3

As soon as we get to the garage I see Harold's feet sticking out from under a Toyota Tacoma. I give his boot a
kick and he drops his wrench on the cement floor and
slides out from under the truck.

His hair is thick, dark brown, and wild. He lets it
stick up all over his head like he just woke up, and that's
only one thing I like about Harold.

"What do we have here?" he asks, standing up and
wiping his hands on his jumpsuit. "Shouldn't you be in
school, Robbie?"

"Got in trouble."

"Trouble is no place to be," he says.

"Better than school." I sit on the stool that has the
one shorter leg that I can always get rocking really good.

From here I have a perfect view of all four bays, and right now each bay is full. And each car has something wrong with it, and I bet I could figure out as fast as anyone how to fix every last one.

"Got busy here this afternoon," Harold tells Grandpa.

Harold is my grandpa's left-hand man. That's because everyone knows I'm Grandpa's right hand. But left-hand man or not, I don't want a lecture from him about school and working hard and being good. He sometimes does that, pulls up a stool and sits down next to me and looks at me right under the brim of my Dodgers hat, right in my eyes, and tells me how I need to get through school and be my best self. Grandpa says it's because Harold and his husband, Paul, are adopting a kid and he's practicing being a dad.

Harold is regular dad age. I bet he hopes when he and Paul get their kid she's not like me. Someone who doesn't get all red hot inside, who doesn't punch stupid boys' noses, even when they deserve it, someone who doesn't make him shake his head for anything.

"So what happened?" Harold asks.

"Had to take care of this boy and his crappy attitude."

Harold tugs one of my braids. "I thought you were working with that counselor at school on not getting so angry. Counting to ten and stuff like that."

"Her name's Ms. Gloria. And I am working on it." Harold was there when Grandpa signed the papers to let me start seeing a counselor at school. That was the last time Grandpa was in the office, and I promised myself I'd never make the school drag him back there. Stupid Alex Carter. "But even if I counted to ten today I still would've slugged him."

He hits the brim of my Dodgers hat, which I usually hate but don't really mind when Harold does it. "Always my little spark plug."

And I know what Harold means, but I'm not his little spark plug. I'm all Grandpa's. He's the only person I'm related to, which is maybe turning out to be a raw deal for him.

Harold throws his arm around my shoulders. "Listen, kid." And I know he's going in for the whole practice dad talk. "When you're out there in the world, you're representing your family. And I know you weren't raised to be fighting."

I nod my head and keep teetering on the stool, hoping that Grandpa has a job for me.

"Little spark plug like her . . ." Harold starts.

"From an old codger like me," Grandpa finishes. That's one of the jokes they're always saying. Like who could ever believe that I came from my grandpa?

We still get that from time to time, even in a town

this small, where almost everyone knows us. Long looks and scrunched-up faces trying to solve our family puzzle.

Sometimes Grandpa reminds me that I'm one-quarter black, even though you can't tell by looking at me. "And that one-quarter comes straight from yours truly," he says, jamming his thick thumb to his chest. It doesn't matter that you can't see it right off, he tells me. That one-quarter is still in me, beneath my surface, deep at my core.

When I was little and didn't understand, I used to picture a shiny, silver twenty-five cents quarter deep in me, next to my heart. Most grandpas pulled quarters from behind little kids' ears and let them go to Dean and Walt's country store for penny candy, and it made me feel better to think that Grandpa's quarter was somewhere deep in me, and worth something more than candy. Worth keeping.

"Up off your duff, Robbie." Grandpa claps his hands twice to get me moving. "We've got work to do."

Harold gives me a fist bump, picks up his wrench, and slides back under the truck. Grandpa tosses me my work gloves, which are just like his but smaller, and points in the direction of the closest bay. I nod and toss my baseball glove on the stool.

"What we've got this afternoon is a 2003 Toyota

4Runner," Grandpa says. But I know that without anyone telling me. I know cars like I know baseball.

I pull on my gloves and Grandpa shows me a box of replacement headlight bulbs.

"You remember how to do it?" he asks.

"Yup." And I know Grandpa remembers too, because even if he sometimes forgets that he already had his morning cup of coffee, or that it's winter so he'll need his jacket, he never forgets cars. That's one place where his memory isn't tired at all. And that's a good thing because I don't need Harold raising his eyebrows and looking long at Grandpa. Harold's too busy to notice anyway. He's always under a car or thinking about his new baby coming soon.

"Ready?" Grandpa asks.

"Ready," I say.

I slide my fingers under the hood of the car and find the lever. When I pull on it, the hood pops up fast like it's been waiting to burst all day. I know what that's like.

Grandpa tests me on the basics before we get started. This is our warm-up. He points. I name.

"This one." He's pointing to a round cap in the middle.

"Check and change oil."

He moves his finger to the right.

"Transmission fluid."

"And here?" His finger points toward the back and I have to stand up on my toes and lean in far to see.

"Washer fluid."

I know them all.

Grandpa pulls on his gloves too, which means we're ready to start the job.

"First?" he asks.

I turn my Dodgers hat backward and look into the hood. I see the connector lock release. "Disconnect the light," I say. Then I do it. Pressing down on the lock release makes a small pop like a short bunt, and I like that. When I pull at it a little, it disconnects from the old, burnt bulb.

Grandpa's hovering over me, making sure I do it right. "Good," he assures me. "Now what?"

"Retaining ring." I stick my head in closer to find it. The faint smell of plastic and metal and oil rise up to my face, and I like that smell. When I find the ring I twist it to the left and detach it from the headlight assembly. Then I take the burnt bulb from the retaining ring and give it to Grandpa. He throws it in the trash.

"Good, Robbie."

I still have the retaining ring around my finger. Grandpa puts the new bulb in my other hand, and I put it exactly where the other one was in the headlight assembly. Then I twist the ring back and it's in. It feels good when everything pops in and fits just right.

"Last?"

"Plug her in!" I shout and reach for the connector socket.

"Ta-da!" Grandpa cheers. "A-plus." An A-plus from Grandpa in the garage is better than any other A-plus ever.

"Now the other one," he says. And I do it all over again, but this time Grandpa doesn't say anything because I know the steps by heart.

When I finish, Grandpa squeezes my shoulder, but in a *good job* kind of way this time, and Harold comes over to start the car and turn the lights on. "Looking bright, Robbie," he says, and reaches out for another fist bump, which is kind of our thing.

I'm not feeling all hot and mad and like I could burst anymore.

In the bay next to us, an intern from the technical high school down the street is working. It's his last day, which is good because he's taking my jobs. Right now he's jump-starting a Honda Accord. I know how to do that too. That's even easier than changing headlights. Grandpa doesn't let me use the word *easy* in the garage, though. He tells me it seems easy because I'm good at it. "If it was easy, why would all these people bring their cars in here to have us do it for them?" he says. I guess that makes Grandpa a genius, then. And me too.

Sparks shoot from the Honda's battery like little tiny fires, and Harold rushes over to help. I know that the little fires mean the intern attached a negative to a positive by accident. Either that or he didn't connect the jumper cables to the dead battery first. Grandpa says that's really important and that those sparks can catch fast. I know how that is too.

But right now I feel pretty OK. Far from Ms. Burg and Alex Carter and his clicky-heeled mom.

There are only three places in the whole world that make me feel like this, like I'm not sparky at all. Third base, where Jackie Robinson played; our sugar maple trees in the backyard; and in Grandpa's garage, fixing something that's broken.

chapter 4

"What do you bet the sap's running?" Grandpa asks when we're walking home from the garage. I bet it's running fast because the conditions are perfect. I also bet he already forgot all about Alex Carter, and about me getting in trouble at school today.

"I think we should be ready to collect," I say. And as soon as we get to our house I throw my book bag and baseball glove on the porch, grab the empty milk jugs from the shed, and shove my feet in my big Bogs boots that come almost up to my knees.

Out back, we have twenty sugar maples that are bigger around than Grandpa's hugs. A few weeks ago we drilled two holes in each, hammered in taps, and attached metal buckets for the sap to drip down into. It started running as soon as we drilled the holes, like the trees had been waiting to burst. That's what happens when you tap them at the exact right time. When it's freezing at night but sunny and warm during the day.

As soon as we get out to the backyard I can see fat drops of sap falling from the taps into the buckets.

"Time to empty." Grandpa hands me a cheesecloth.

We have to filter the sap from the metal buckets through a piece of cheesecloth to collect all the bad stuff so it doesn't get mixed in.

We run the sap through the filters and collect it in the old plastic jugs. Once they're full, it's my job to half bury the jugs at the edge of our yard and pack them tight in the snow to keep the sap cool.

Grandpa says we'll boil soon.

"If you promise to be good at school tomorrow, you can help me split," he says.

I don't technically say I promise, but I know I'll be good enough to keep Ms. Burg from calling Grandpa in. I don't want anyone else asking him questions and telling him how bad I've been and making him shake his head and rub his temples. No way. I can be good enough to keep Grandpa away from all those adults and all their concerns.

I run back to the shed for our work gloves and protective glasses and Grandpa's ax. The snow in the yard is halfway up my boots, and I like the way it feels to sink in all the way to my rolled-up jeans as I walk back to Grandpa. He only lets me hold the ax with the head down and with two hands, and only if I walk.

It's my job to put the big pieces of wood on the old stump chopping block. I have to place them perfectly so they don't wobble at all. It's Grandpa's job to swing the ax and split the wood along the grain into smaller pieces that'll fit in our outdoor fire pit for when we start to boil the sap down into syrup.

Grandpa always breathes out a big "Ha!" when he swings the ax down on the wood, like an umpire calling a strike. Then the wood cracks like a broken bat, split down the grain. Sometimes it only takes one hit like that and the wood just falls apart. Sometimes it's a little tougher. Like if the wood has a big knot in it, the ax can't get through it right off and Grandpa has to take lots of swings and then pry it apart with his hands at the end.

"Couple more," Grandpa says, and I know he's getting tired because he's not pulling the ax up as high over his head as he did the first time. But his memory's not tired. Not out here. He never forgets what he's doing at his chopping block, like his brain is hardwired. Hardwired to fix broken cars and split wood out by our sugar maples.

And I sometimes wonder if he remembers other things out here at the chopping block while his memory isn't so bad. Like my mom. And the way her voice sounded and if I look like her or what happened that made him shut up so tight like his tongue forgot how to say her name.

And I'm thinking about asking him. Trying again while we're out here at the chopping block. I run my work glove against the rough bark of the next piece of wood and open my mouth, but I know he'll just shake his head and change the subject. Like he always does.

"OK, Robbie," he says. "That'll do for tonight." He lowers his ax and I lob the new split pieces on the stack under the eaves of the house.

The creases are deep across his forehead, and I hope that he is remembering all that stuff out here by the sugar maples, because no matter how deep I search, no matter how hard I think, or how tight I close my eyes and try to see, I'll never be able to find any memories. And I'm scared he's forgetting his. Then I'll never know.

I make footsteps in the snow for Grandpa to follow, and I wait behind him on the porch as he struggles with the key to the front door, pushing the wrong one in over and over even when it doesn't fit. "Goddammit!" he grunts. "This stupid . . ."

I put my hand over his. "This one, Grandpa." I point

to the silver key hanging on the chain. "That big one's for the garage, remember?"

"Of course I remember that," he says.

I smile up at him and know that even if I try to ask now, it's too late, because he's all jumbled up and confused. But there's no one else to tell me about her, so I help Grandpa up the steps and into the warm house.

chapter 5

When I get to school the next day everyone's looking at me funny. They always kind of do because I'm the only girl they know who wears boy clothes and kicks everyone's butt at baseball, but today they're looking at me extra funny, like Alex's blood is still sprayed up my sleeve or something. I hop over the wooden fence into the schoolyard and don't pay them no mind. Just like Jackie Robinson.

"They let her back here?" I hear one girl scoff.

"No way." It's Chelsea and Brittany. They're completely pink from their Uggs all the way to the gum they're smacking with every stupid syllable they say. They're also the girls who hang off Alex Carter like he's some god or something.

"I can't believe it. Did you see what she did to Alex?"

"Shouldn't she be suspended? Her grandpa came and picked her up. If that even is her grandpa."

My hand makes a fist, but I just let the words run right off, like Grandpa says. And I try to count to ten while I'm searching around for Derek because I usually hang with him until the doors open for school. I put my baseball glove up over my mouth like I'm talking secret messages on the mound with my pitcher and catcher and blow hot air in the leather pocket. Each breath warms up my face before it fades back to cold.

Then I see him running across the yard and yelling my name. "Rob!" Derek looks so funny when he runs that he's making me laugh right out loud into my glove. He's stick skinny and short and his ears kind of poke out, but his feet are so big that he looks like he might trip over them at any second. He can tell I'm laughing at him too, but he doesn't mind because he knows we're cool. Ever since I peeled off the *kick the midget* Post-it that Alex Carter stuck on his back in third grade, he's been kind of hanging around. And that's OK with me.

"Rob! Rob!" He's yelling and waving his hands over his head.

He's not named after Derek Jeter either. He didn't even know who that was when I asked. He doesn't know anything about baseball. Watching him running over toward me, I'm thinking we should switch names, Derek and me, because he's as soft and small as a Robin and I'm as hard as a Derek. That *k* like the crack of a bat. *K* for *strike*. I'm hard like that. He's the one that's like feathers. I guess that's why we're friends.

He's all out of breath by the time he gets to me. "Did you get in trouble?" he huffs.

"Not enough. I'm still here, aren't I?" I punch my right fist into my third baseman's glove.

"I've been wanting to see that kid get slammed since first grade." He's still breathing hard as anything. "His nose exploded!"

"I know. I'm the one who exploded it," I remind him. "No one calls me a motherless Robin bird."

Derek goes quiet, and I know that means he's sorry Alex was such a jerk. "What did your grandpa say?"

"Same stuff my grandpa always tells me. That I have to be more like Jackie Robinson." Even though Grandpa didn't say anything about Jackie Robinson to me at all this time, like it didn't matter anymore who I was named for.

"Well, Alex Carter deserved to get popped." He looks around the yard. "Think he'll come today?" he asks.

I shrug my shoulders. "Doubt it. He was crying like a baby."

Derek gives me a high five as the bell rings and

everyone runs toward the big double doors of the school.

Principal Wheeler is directing us into our class lines in the lobby while we wait for our teachers. We get in the back of Ms. Meg's homeroom line, and I'm looking for Alex, but I don't see him, which is kind of too bad because I want to see what his nose looks like after a day of bruising. I bet it's purple and yellow and gross. I want everyone to see what a nose looks like after you call me a motherless Robin bird.

"Hey, Robinson." It's Candace, a girl from our class, and she's tapping me on my shoulder. She's a little pink too, but not the gum-smacky kind of pink that Chelsea and Brittany are.

"You OK?" she asks. "I saw the whole thing, how Alex was making fun of you yesterday even after you told him to stop."

"I'm fine," I say.

She starts kicking the snow out of her Bogs, which are the same boots I wear sugaring except hers are pink and mine are black. Then she says, "I think Alex is a huge jerk. I just wanted to tell you that. And no one ever stands up to him and I'm glad you did."

Candace looks up from her boots and is smiling really big and holding her hand up for a high five like Derek does sometimes. I give it to her and it feels pretty OK.

"Are you grounded or anything?" she asks. "My mom would have died if she knew I hit someone."

The words stick in me sharp, a fastball in the gut, and I can tell she feels bad the second she says it because she looks down at her Bogs again.

Derek grabs my wrist. But I shake him off. I'm not a touching kind of person like that.

I imagine shoving Candace. Just a little maybe so she remembers not to complain about her mom around me because at least her mom isn't actually dead, but I shake the image out of my head and start counting to ten instead.

"I'm not in trouble," I mutter.

"I'm glad," Candace says to her Bogs.

Then I turn around fast and hope the line starts moving down the hall to Ms. Meg's room.

"You wanted to punch her, didn't you?" Derek whispers.

"Shut up or I'll punch you," I whisper back, but Derek knows I'm not serious because I wouldn't ever have to punch him.

"She was trying to be nice, you know," he says.

And I do know. That's why I didn't shove her. That's why I counted to ten like Ms. Gloria taught me and remembered some baseball stats. *Career saves: Mariano Rivera, 652.*

Finally Ms. Meg shows up and we start walking to homeroom. Derek nudges me. "Remember. What would Jackie do?" and that gets him cracking up right away. He always laughs when he says that, like it's the funniest thing he's ever come up with. It is kind of funny, I guess, but not too funny because I actually have to ask myself that sometimes.

Today, Jackie would just stand in line and get through the day. So that's what I'm going to do.

chapter 6

Ms. Gloria's been pulling me out of class for counseling once a week on Wednesdays almost the whole year. It started as soon as Ms. Meg and Mr. Danny noticed that I boil over easier than a pot of sap. But today's not Wednesday, it's Friday, and she's knocking on Ms. Meg's door and I know even before she pokes her head in that I'm going to have to go with her right now anyway.

"Robinson?" She waves me over.

Ms. Gloria's hair is wavy with curls and already turning white. She pulls it back in a loose small bun at the back of her head, but the curls creep out and spill down the sides of her face. Her eyes are blue. Not baby-blanket wussy blue like Alex Carter's, they're windshield-washer-fluid blue. Like they could scrub-the-streaks-and-smudges-and-bird-crap-right-out-of-you blue. And when she looks straight into your eyes and uses her no-nonsense voice, there's nothing anybody can really do but what she says.

"Bring your stuff," Ms. Gloria tells me. When she turns away, I roll my eyes and try to take three deep breaths because when I bring my stuff that means it's not going to be quick, and next period we have recess and that's the best period of the day and I'm going to have to spend it reading with Ms. Gloria. Or talking about my feelings. Which is about the opposite of a game of snow baseball.

I drag my book bag behind me along the classroom floor and walk as slowly as I can because more time walking means less time talking about my feelings. I look back at Derek and he gives me a goofy grin. Candace's head is down on the desk and I wonder if she still feels bad about telling me her mom would die if she hit someone, or if there's something else making her head heavy. But she picks it up and half smiles too and sends me a little secret thumbs-up. I half smile back. Maybe quarter smile.

"You're going to have recess with me today," Ms. Gloria says as we walk down the hall, like it's some prize. "And we're going to chat about taking some responsibility for your actions."

"Are you going to have recess with Alex when he comes back, to tell him to stop being a huge jerk?"

"Alex will have consequences for his own behavior."

"Yeah, like a broken face."

"Robinson." Ms. Gloria's using her no-nonsense voice, and she stops me right there in the hall and makes me turn my Dodgers hat around backward so I have to look straight into her washer-fluid-blue eyes. "I'm not saying Alex was right. But I am saying you were wrong." Then she starts walking again and calls over her shoulder, "And *keep* that hat out of your eyes. I don't want to suggest to Principal Wheeler that we revisit our hat policy."

What would Jackie do? I ask real quiet in my head, and it's kind of hard because I think he might run down the hall to join his class lining up outside Ms. Meg's room to go to recess. I think he might tell Ms. Gloria that she couldn't stop him because he had third base to protect and a batting average to raise up.

"Can't we do this after—"

"Nope," she answers and opens the door to her small room. It has space for one long table, six chairs, Ms. Gloria's desk in the corner, and lots of posters on the walls about feelings and "accountable talk" and "I statements" and other warm fuzzy stupid stuff, and a couple of bookshelves with bins full of books. I sometimes take books from the bin that says *sports*. Ms. Meg says I should read all different kinds of books, but Ms. Gloria says I can read whatever I want in her room.

I sit down where I always sit, staring out the only window into the yard and I can tell Ms. Gloria is looking right at me because my hat is still turned backward and I know if I try to pull it back over my face she'll make me turn it right back around, or take it until the end of the day, or even tattle to Principal Wheeler. So I just forget it. But that doesn't mean I have to look at her.

"Tell me about what happened yesterday."

At first I stay shut, but I know that doesn't work with Ms. Gloria because once she waited me out all the way through lunch and recess. I had to eat this gross brown bag lunch brought up by the cafeteria lady with an icy milk and smushed jelly sandwich that didn't even have peanut butter because Alex Carter is allergic so no one can have peanut butter in our school ever. He ruins everything.

So I grumble, "Yesterday was fine."

She just keeps waiting, which means that my answer isn't good enough, so she'll wait until I say something that she calls "real."

"Robin isn't my name," I say, and even thinking about Alex Carter jumping around me and flapping his arms is getting me all mad again and my fists clench up. "I told him to stop. I told him to call me my real name and that I'm not any feathery little Robin bird. I'm Robinson, and my grandpa gave me that name on purpose, so he better shut up."

"Do you want to tell me about your name, or about your grandpa?"

I cross my arms over my chest and sit back in my chair, staring down at my rolled-up jeans and Nike Air Griffeys. "No."

"Then let's look at this." Ms. Gloria pulls out a piece of paper with my name at the top and *Behavior Plan* typed out in big letters, a list of directions, and a picture of a baseball diamond with all the bases.

"Ms. Meg, Mr. Danny, and I put this together so you can track your own behavior and start joining your classmates again for recess."

"Is Alex getting one of these?"

"His business is not your business," Ms. Gloria says. "You can only change your own behavior."

She taps her finger on the behavior plan. Each base of the baseball diamond is supposed to be a part of the school day. Morning is first base, lunch and recess are second base, and afternoon is third base. Ms. Gloria explains how Ms. Meg and Mr. Danny will give me a score for each and my goal is to make it to home base every day.

Stupid.

Through the window I can see the other kids in my class roll the bodies of snowmen across the yard. Mr. Danny is handing out baseballs and bats, and a couple of guys throw down their black book bags to make visible bases for snow baseball. It's not fair that they're playing when no one in this school would have even had the idea to play baseball in the winter if it weren't for me, and I'm stuck in here because I showed a bully what happens when you're mean to Robinson Hart.

"Robinson." Ms. Gloria snaps her fingers and points at the behavior plan again. "On the top of the page is a reminder list of all the things you're working on." Then she makes me read my goals out loud.

"One: use appropriate language for school. Two: count to ten, take three deep breaths, or recite baseball stats in my head to calm down when I'm feeling angry. Three: socialize with others by asking them questions about themselves," I mumble.

"What do you think?" Ms. Gloria asks. And I want to tell her that this piece of paper isn't going to make any bit of difference at all and that I belong at recess hitting real home runs out in the snow and not fake home runs on this dumb baseball diamond drawing.

But because I hate missing recess and I don't want Grandpa to ever have to go to the principal's office again or Harold to have to give me another practice dad speech, I say, "It's fine." And for a second I think maybe from now on I can just make up my mind to be good.

"You had a big strike yesterday," Ms. Gloria reminds me. "I expect a home run from you today."

Then I see Alex through the window. He's running across the yard toward the snow baseball game. I lean forward trying to see what his nose looks like. I can't tell from this tiny room, but he's high-fiving Ronald in left field and hustling to take his place in center.

"What the—Alex is here?" I blurt.

"OK, let's think of a strategy for reentering your class this afternoon," Ms. Gloria says. "Especially since your favorite person has arrived."

She's trying to be funny, and I'm trying to come up with a plan, but all I can think about is Alex in the outfield and how no one is making him stay in from recess even though he started everything, and how it really isn't Candace's fault that she mentioned her mom like that and how I should be nicer to her.

And I'm trying to listen to Ms. Gloria, but really I'm thinking about how Derek is just sitting off to the side of the baseball game outside, blowing on a snowball he made, watching it melt between his mittens like he always does, and I have to be inside and he isn't even playing. We shouldn't just switch names, we should switch lives, because he'd probably love to stay inside and talk about his feelings with Ms. Gloria instead of going to recess, and then I could beam a line drive right in the hole between Alex and Ronald in the outfield.

Ms. Gloria raps her knuckles on the table in front of me. "Robbie, can you tell me what I just said?" The words didn't stick at all. I was trying, I swear, but my mind was running the bases somewhere else.

And then Alex catches an inning-ender fly ball and is pumping his fist and trotting toward home. He nudges Ronald, who's running next to him, and points toward Derek, who is still sitting on the sidelines, not paying attention to the game because I'm not playing, and there's no one else for him to hang with. Then Alex nudges Ronald again and points and jogs up close to Derek, and lobs the ball right at Derek's head. It glances his cheek and shocks him half to death because he grabs his face and rolls backward like the stick-skinny little kid he is and I'm pretty sure he's crying because he hates sports and scares easy. And Alex and Ronald are laughing and pointing at him and making it worse, so other kids laugh too.

And Mr. Danny is blowing his whistle, not because he saw what Alex did and is calling a foul, but because recess is over and it's time for everyone to run through the doors to the lunchroom.

And before I know it my fists are clenched and my

jaw is locked and I'm sprinting away from Ms. Gloria and her little room and the baseball diamond behavior plan and flying through the big double doors, down the hallway, and into the lunchroom. And I'm trying to count to ten or take three deep breaths, but it feels like jumper cables are clamping down hard, positive is attaching to negative, and sparks are about to fly.

And before I know it, I'm locked up arm in arm with Alex Carter and pulling his stupid soft feather hair hard and pushing him down to the lunchroom floor. He's trying to get away and swinging punches toward my face but he's not strong enough and I've got him pinned, staring at his ugly bruised-up nose, and I'm thinking that I'm glad Ms. Gloria made me pull my hat around backward because now I can get even more up in his face like when the coach springs from the dugout and argues with the ump. And I want to punch him again hard for what he did to Derek at recess because Derek is small and never did anything to hurt anyone, but I don't want Grandpa coming back here. So just as I'm trying to think of baseball stats—*Hit by pitch, Alex Rodriguez, 175 times*—and realizing that Alex Carter is just like Alex Rodriguez, acting all tough and perfect but really such a sissy-boy cheater, Mr. Danny is blowing his whistle and pulling me off Alex.

Chelsea and Brittany are standing with their lunch

trays pressed against their stupid pink sweaters and their mouths are hanging open, staring.

Kids are circling around and Mr. Danny's trying to keep me separate from Alex and get me to walk toward the lunchroom doors. "What do you think you're doing?" he's shouting.

And Derek is running up and yelling, "She was helping me! See what he did?" and showing off the red mark on his cold skin where Alex lobbed the ball at his cheek. "Alex is a bully! No one ever sees it!"

And Alex Carter is crying on the floor and holding his head and acting all innocent.

I try to shake out of Mr. Danny's grip because his voice has gotten softer and serious and he's talking right to me. "Why did you do that? Robinson, why did you do that?" He's all up in my face. And I don't like him all up in my face like that, and I don't like that Ms. Gloria rushed to the lunchroom too but is kneeling down by Alex and helping him up when she's supposed to be on my team. So I stomp hard on Mr. Danny's foot and tell him to back off and that he doesn't know crap about me. But he doesn't loosen his grip. He drags me off to the principal's office and points to the same chair I was in yesterday and says to Ms. Burg, "Bring in her grandpa again."

Derek's outside the office door and I can see him

through the window and he's trying to explain to Ms. Gloria what happened and he's pointing to his cheek. She pats him on the shoulder, sends him to the nurse, comes in the office, and looks straight at me with her stern, disappointed face. And before I can tell her that I remembered a baseball stat instead of punching Alex Carter in the face again even though he deserved it, she says, "Strike two, Robbie."

chapter 7

This time when Grandpa hobbles his side-to-side walk into the office Harold is with him, which means Grandpa is going to shake his head and I'm going to get a practice dad talk. And I wish Harold would just save it for his own kid because I didn't do anything wrong.

Grandpa's mad. He grabs my arm hard and squeezes until I can feel my heart beat in his hand. "What were you thinking?"

I'm not used to seeing Grandpa mad, and it looks all wrong on him.

"Let go," I say and yank my arm away. I've never been mad at Grandpa before either, and that feels all wrong too, but he was squeezing my arm and glaring at me like I was in big trouble and he never even asked me what happened.

"You have some explaining to do," he says.

"Whatever," I mumble.

That makes him glare harder, so I pull the brim of my hat down and he says, "Not whatever."

Harold is shaking hands with Ms. Gloria and Mr. Danny and if they didn't already know better, everyone would think he's my dad because my family's so messed up and I don't look like anyone or act like anyone I know and everyone just shakes their heads and wishes I belonged to someone else.

Principal Wheeler opens her office door. "Please come in," she says. "We only have a few minutes before the teachers need to get back to their classrooms."

Then everyone's walking past me and into her office. Ms. Gloria, Ms. Meg, Mr. Danny, Grandpa, and Harold. They'll all say how frustrated they are with me and come up with some plan as brilliant as a baseball diamond drawn out on a piece of paper. This time I scoot to the chair closest to Principal Wheeler's door so I can press my ear up and try to hear what crap they're saying about me, and if Grandpa's finishing his sentences, because it's afternoon and I'm making him stressed and his memory might get tired. And I can't have anyone looking at him long and wondering if he's unfit to raise a girl like me. Because he's not.

"Robinson," Ms. Burg huffs and motions for me to move away from the door, but I stare at her like no way am I moving just because she told me to, and she looks the other way and shakes her head too.

It's hard to catch everything, but I can hear Grandpa saying he's sorry over and over. And I don't know if it's because he's really that sorry or if he forgets he already said it. And it's not even him who should be sorry. Alex Carter should be in there saying sorry over and over for being so mean to kids half his size. And calling me Robin and motherless, then acting all innocent.

I can hear Mr. Danny's tone through the door, which is mad and annoyed, probably because both times I fought Alex Carter have been when he was in charge of the yard, so it makes him look pretty bad. But no one could've stopped me, so he shouldn't even really feel that bad either.

And I hear Ms. Gloria saying, "We need to hold on to her. I'm worried. It has to be a group effort."

And I hear Ms. Meg saying, "A suspension site would be horrible for Robinson right now." And all this other stuff about hearings and legal representation. And it's starting to seem pretty serious. I want to be suspended, but suspended to Grandpa's garage to figure out what's wrong with all the cars, and suspended to our backyard to help Grandpa split wood and boil sap. I don't know what a suspension site is, but it sounds bad.

I slide my Dodgers hat back around over my face and press my ear closer to the door.

Harold is asking, "If Charlie signs this, what exactly is he agreeing to?" And Ms. Gloria's talking about how she pulls me out on Wednesdays for counseling already and something else I can't hear. And something about anger, and my goals, and talking.

And then it's kind of quiet and I picture them all shaking their heads. Grandpa says he's sorry again and Harold says thank you to everyone. And I quickly move back to the other chair so it doesn't seem like I was spying.

"Robinson, please come in here." It's Principal Wheeler's voice. When I walk in, Grandpa can hardly look at me, which is fine because I still have my hat pulled down far.

"Turn that hat around." Ms. Gloria means business. She'll wait me out, so I just do, but I make a big huff about it because I like my hat the way I like it.

"We are all really worried about you, Robbie," she says. I hate that crap. No one needs to worry about me but myself. "Your behavior is unacceptable. It's troubling, we don't like it, and it can't happen anymore." Ms.

Gloria is using her no-nonsense voice. "We're going to be watching you like a hawk and trying to get to the bottom of this. Ms. Meg's going to be watching, Mr. Danny is, your grandpa will be too, and you know I'll be watching you."

"Me too, Robbie." Harold pats my shoulder. "I've got my eye on you too."

He's trying to be all practice dad. And I want to tell everyone that the only one who needs to be watching me is Grandpa because I'm his and no one else's.

"So I'm not going to be suspended?"

"No," Principal Wheeler answers.

They're just going to make my life here crappier by being up in my business.

"The first thing you'll do is figure out a way to apologize to Alex. Consider it your weekend homework," Ms. Gloria tells me.

"You can't be serious—"

"Very serious, Robbie. Your actions were very serious and now we are all very serious."

"Are you going to make him apologize to Derek?"

Then Grandpa reaches across the table and grabs my arm again, but not hard. Like he's just holding me still for a minute. "You'll apologize." He takes a deep breath. "And you'll do what . . ." And I can see Grandpa's searching for his words and I hate the look on his face when that happens, like he's wandered off and gotten lost and can't find his way back to what he was saying.

". . . what Ms. Gloria says," I finish. "I'll do what Ms. Gloria says." And it kills me to say that because I don't want to do what Ms. Gloria says, but it kills me more to leave Grandpa hanging in the middle of his sentence with everyone watching.

Ms. Gloria starts explaining about how I'm still going to be seeing her but with a small group of other kids, and I want to yell that there's no way I'm doing that but Grandpa's hand is there holding me still so I remember some stats until Ms. Gloria is done talking and Harold is shaking everyone's hand again.

"Let's go," Grandpa says. He keeps holding my arm as we walk out of the school like I might run if he lets go. And even though running fast and hard across the yard right now would make me feel better, I'd never run from Grandpa.

Harold is walking a half step ahead of us, and it's not until then that I realize they must have closed the garage because of me, and now there are going to be so many cars to catch up on. At least I can help with that.

That's when I hear the clicky heels approaching down the sidewalk. "It's Alex's mom," I whisper to Harold, and I pull my hat back around to cover my face.

"Mrs. Carter?" Harold reaches out for a handshake,

but she doesn't even look at Harold, she looks straight under the brim of my Dodgers hat with those grooves carving deep across her forehead.

"I'm Haro—" he tries, but she cuts him off quick.

"I thought I told you to keep your hands off Alex."

Grandpa gives my arm a squeeze. "What do you say, Robbie?"

"Sorry," I mutter. "He was bullying my friend, and I couldn't let that happen."

"Don't put this on him," she spurts. "He has enough to deal with. Next time you go near him I will be pressing charges." She clicks off into the school and down the hall toward the nurse's office, where I'm sure Alex is playing his innocent-pretty-boy routine.

"What's pressing charges?" I ask.

"Lawyers. Lawyers and big trouble," Harold explains.

And that shuts me up fast because I don't need other people's moms and teachers and definitely not lawyers sticking their noses in our business.

"You've really done it this time," Grandpa mumbles and nudges me down the street.

Harold shakes Grandpa's hand and tells me that we have a big talk coming. Then he turns toward the garage and Grandpa points the other way down the street toward home.

"We're not going to the garage?" I ask. But he doesn't

even answer me or tell me one crap thing about Jackie Robinson and how hard it was for him to stay calm when everyone was acting terrible. He just keeps holding my arm and walking as fast as his side-to-side legs can go.

"I can help with all the extra cars from today—"

"That's enough, Robbie," Grandpa cuts me off, and keeps on walking.

When we get home and go up the steps Grandpa tries two keys that don't fit, the one for the garage and the one for the truck. I don't help him or say a word because I'm so mad we're not at the garage sealing transmissions or replacing brake pads.

When the right key finally slides in, Grandpa goes straight to his office, where the mail is piled up, brings out a piece of paper and pen, and tells me to sit at the kitchen table.

"Write your apology to that boy."

"Alex? No way." I shove the paper away. But Grandpa's not even listening because he's mad at me just like I'm mad at him.

The door slams and Grandpa's gone out in the yard. I can see him through the kitchen window, and I can't believe he's collecting sap in the jugs without me. And he's putting the big pieces of wood on the stump chopping block by himself and swinging the ax up high and down hard to split them through the middle, and he does each piece in one fast swing. The two halves just break apart, easy as that.

I crumple the blank paper and cross my arms over my chest. But I can hear each hard thwack of the ax and each "Ha!" that Grandpa grunts when he makes contact, and every one makes me grit my teeth harder because I want to check how many gallons we got and I want to throw the split pieces on the woodpile.

And before I know it, dark is creeping up outside and I can't hear him thwacking anymore. I'm looking out the window and I can't see him at the chopping block or the sap buckets. I stand up and peer around to the woodpile, but he's not there stacking either. All the split wood is just lying around the stump where it fell.

I'm shoving my feet in my boots and not even zipping my jacket because something feels wrong. Grandpa never gets mad and he never leaves chopped wood scattered, and a bad feeling is sitting hard in my stomach.

I swing open the door and yell, "Grandpa!" I can hear my voice echo off the sky through the woods. I run past the stump chopping block and our gallons of sap packed in the snow, following Grandpa's side-to-side footprints right past the metal hanging buckets and dripping sap and into the woods. "Grandpa!" My breath is hanging in the dark, cold air. "Grandpa!"

I'm wondering if he decided to go on our favorite hike on the Appalachian Trail that runs behind our yard and up to the hiker shelter, where we stop to eat lunch on summer weekends. But he wouldn't go without me. And he wouldn't go at night or in the winter. Without the first aid kit and without a headlamp.

My heart is beating fast because maybe he forgot it was winter. Or maybe he forgot where the trail goes. Or maybe he's that mad at me, and he's running away.

I hear a crunch of snow and I trudge after it, following his prints farther into the woods. "Grandpa!"

And then he's calling back out to me. "Robbie?" With that voice full of gravel. "Here!"

And he's just standing there, leaning against the trunk of a tree, and his eyes are big like when we catch a deer in the headlights of the truck. Like he's scared.

"Grandpa?"

"I guess I just got a little turned around," he says. "I thought we tapped some more maples back here, no?"

"No, Grandpa." I walk up to him slow like he really is a deer who might scare off easy and forever if I'm not careful. I take the ax from him and hold it head down and with two hands like he taught me. "Follow me," I say and make him hold on to my shoulder as we tramp back through the woods toward the house until we get to the yard.

I can't let the chopped wood stay all scattered in the snow. And seeing it like that makes me wish I could take it all back again. Like Grandpa could pull the ax out of those pieces he split, and put them back together, and I could pull back my shove from Alex's shoulders and run back into the room with Ms. Gloria and just talk about my feelings because if I had then I wouldn't have weighed down Grandpa's engine like that, I wouldn't have made his memory tired, and he wouldn't have wandered off without me.

Grandpa and I pick up the pieces and stack them with the rest, and I promise myself for real this time, I'll be more like Jackie Robinson.

chapter 8

It's Monday and I have a blank copy of the baseball diamond behavior plan so I can get around my bases by the end of the day, and I'm all ready to start fresh and let things roll right off and stay out of everyone's face, especially Alex Carter's, when Ms. Meg says we're going to do a project about our family trees.

She can forget about that right now, because I'm not doing it. No way.

Alex starts whispering something to Ronald, and I bet it's something mean. They're laughing and Ms. Meg gives them a look, so they stop. But when she turns away Alex goes back to whispering and laughing and he's rolling up tiny little paper balls and tossing them into Oscar's dark curly hair in front of him. It's making me all hot and mad because he doesn't have some stupid baseball diamond plan out on his desk to help him not be a jerk.

Already I regret writing him an apology this weekend, even though I wrote it as a haiku, which Ms. Meg told us is the earliest form of poetry. But that's not why I chose it. I chose it because it's short.

Alex, I'm sorry.
That is all I have to say.
That was the last time.

Ms. Meg also taught us that you can interpret poetry in lots of different ways, so while most people think the last line means I won't hit him again, you could also interpret it to mean that I won't apologize again.

But watching him laughing now with Ronald I'm wishing I never crumpled the apology haiku and tossed it in his cubby this morning because he doesn't deserve to read it and he isn't sorry about anything at all. And neither am I.

I ask to go to the bathroom and maybe when I come back I'll have missed the whole project and everyone will be done and presenting their family trees to the class and Ms. Meg will say, *It's OK, Robinson, you don't have to do it because we're moving on to the next thing.* Then we'll just go on to a different project and I'll keep on being cool and letting things roll right off like Jackie Robinson and I'll get through the morning just fine and Ms. Meg will draw a smiley face on first base and send me off to recess with Mr. Danny.

Even though I take extra long in the bathroom and make laps around the fifth-grade floor, peeking my head in other homerooms to see if they're doing stupid family trees too, which I can't tell, when I get back Ms. Meg is still just explaining the project.

"You get to create your family tree however you want," Ms. Meg tells us. Brittany and Chelsea are whispering about papier-mâché at the table behind me, and I picture sticking it across their mouths and letting it harden so all their stupid words are stuck inside their mouths forever and they can never giggle at Alex Carter again.

"Today we'll start by doing a little writing just to get some ideas flowing about our families."

Everyone is unzipping their book bags and taking out their notebooks like they're excited to get started. Except me. Ms. Meg says my name and gives me a look like she's trying to remind me that I'm only one strike away from serious trouble. I yank hard on the zipper of my book bag. My notebook is tucked in the pocket of my baseball glove, which makes me even more mad because

I wish it were recess.

Candace has her head down on the table again, which is weird because she doesn't seem like the head-down-on-the-table type of kid. I guess this project is so stupid that even the good students like Candace don't want to do it.

Ms. Meg makes her way over and pats Candace on the back.

She sits up fast and whispers, "Sorry."

Derek nudges my elbow. "Rob, you OK?" He's really good at knowing when something's wrong. "I can help you—"

"I'm fine," I say, because he can't help. Not with this.

Ms. Meg has her notebook projected up on the Smart Board. It says *Family Tree: Quick Writes*.

Quick Writes are basically writing prompts Ms. Meg gives us. They're usually not so bad because we never have to write too much or for too long, but these ones will be bad.

Derek nudges me again and looks at me like he wants to know if I'm really OK, and I shake him off because I'm trying my best not to be mad at him just because his family tree will probably be easy to make and have lots of branches.

"Number one. I want you to write a list of three people who are important in your family," Ms. Meg says.

I clench down hard on my back teeth and try to remember as many baseball stats as I can. *Career leader, stolen bases: Rickey Henderson, 1,406. Single-season leader, home runs: Barry Bonds, 73, 2001.* But Ms. Meg is giving me that look, so I start writing really slow:

Important People in My Family:
Grandpa

"I have seven so far," someone whispers. And I'm trying to let it roll right off. I can see Derek's list growing longer and longer in my peripheral vision, like I'm a pitcher and he's got a good lead off first base.

"Next question," Ms. Meg announces finally. "This time we'll write for two minutes without stopping." Kids moan, not because they only have one family member, but because they don't want to write for two minutes straight.

"Number two," she says. "Jot down any details you know of your birth. What have your family members told you about the day you were born? Ready? Set. Write." And she starts the timer for two minutes.

Most career ejections of a MLB manager: Bobby Cox, 158. But it doesn't work because before I know it I'm standing up and about to turn the whole table over because this is such crap and I'm not making some stupid family tree project. And everyone is biting their pencils and writing their stories and sketching these gigantic trees with moms and dads and cousins and branches sticking out everywhere and I wish I had Grandpa's ax, because I'd raise it up high over my head and chop them all down in one big swing.

"Robbie." Derek's tugging on my arm, trying to get me to sit back down before I do something stupid.

But then the door creaks open and everyone looks and it's Ms. Gloria, and it's the first time I'm hoping she takes me, because if she doesn't I'm going to break something.

"Robinson," she says calm and low. "You look ready." I'm thinking, *Perfect timing*, when she calls out, "Also, Candace, Oscar, and Alex. You'll be coming with us too."

chapter 9

This has to be some kind of joke. Like a really bad, unfunny joke.

We're all sitting around Ms. Gloria's table in her little room. Alex is across from me. Kicking distance. Candace is next to me, and across from her is Oscar. His hair is still full of those little balled-up pieces of paper that Alex was throwing at him in Ms. Meg's room. Ms. Gloria sits at the head of the table.

"You can't keep me in here with her." Alex pouts and points at me. He has a Band-Aid across his nose.

"Scared?" I ask.

Ms. Gloria's giving us that look that tells us to cut the crap. "You done?"

Alex and I both cross our arms and slump back in

our chairs. Ms. Gloria gives me the sign to turn my hat backward, so I jerk it around hard.

"Good," Ms. Gloria says, all no-nonsense. "Then we can start."

She holds a wand in front of her that has purple and silver glitter floating slowly from the top to the bottom, then she turns it back over and the glitter starts falling again slowly, top to bottom. "This wand holds a lot of power," she tells us.

I'm waiting for someone to break through the door and say they've made a mistake and that I don't have to sit across from Alex Carter ever again in my life and that Ms. Gloria is not about to put a spell on us with some stupid sparkly wand.

"All the students who have ever participated in Group Guidance have held this wand when they speak up and share their feelings in the conversation," she explains. "That's why it's so powerful. There are a lot of words and emotions and bravery captured in here."

"Group Guidance?" I scoff.

Ms. Gloria tells us how we'll be meeting in this group at least three times a week and how the wand is the talking wand and no one speaks unless they are holding it. I want to grab it from her so I can say, *Is this for real? You put me in a group with Alex?*

Ms. Gloria can make me sit here, but there is no way

I'm sharing any words or emotions or bravery or whatever else. If I just stay shut and refuse, maybe they'll rethink my suspension so I can go do something worthwhile like help Grandpa in the garage.

Ms. Gloria rips off a piece of chart paper and uncaps a black marker. I can smell its licorice from here. I hate licorice. "Before we begin, we have to make some rules together. Then once we make the rules, we have to promise to stick to them."

She writes *Group Guidance Norms* across the top of the chart paper.

"Ideas? Anyone?"

Candace starts. "Don't talk unless you have the wand. Respect the wand." I roll my eyes even though I'm trying to be nicer to her. Why does she need to be in Group Guidance anyway? Because she puts her head down on the table sometimes? She's probably the nice kid they threw in with us so we wouldn't fail. Teachers always put a good kid in every group. Otherwise crap never gets done.

Ms. Gloria writes down *Respect the wand!* on the chart paper.

"Respect each other too," Candace adds. "No laughing at what someone says."

Ms. Gloria writes that one down. "Anyone else?"

I look at Oscar and realize I don't think I've heard

him say one word since Ms. Meg introduced him to our class the day he moved here from Brooklyn. That's where the Dodgers are from, but when the Dodgers moved they went to Los Angeles, not to Vermont like Oscar. I don't know why he has to be here either. Maybe every group needs a good kid who raises her hand a lot like Candace and a quiet kid like Oscar who will balance everything out.

Alex is the bully. And I'm the kid who won't let him get away with it.

"Robinson?" Ms. Gloria asks. "What do you think is important to a group conversation? Can you add to our list?"

I want to tell her that I don't think group conversations are important at all, but I just sit there.

Ms. Gloria would wait me out forever because that's what she does, but Candace jumps in. "Eye contact!" Ms. Gloria writes it down.

By the end we have a list. Candace basically created the whole thing, but Ms. Gloria makes us read it over together and sign it on the bottom, which means that we agree to stick to the norms. The list looks like this:

GROUP GUIDANCE NORMS
1. **Respect the wand!**
2. **Respect each other. No laughing at anyone else.**

3. **Use eye contact when someone is speaking.**
4. **Be present. Listen to what others are saying even if you're not sharing.**
5. **Everything we say stays in the room.**
6. **Passing is OK.**

alex carter
Candace Barnes
Oscar Oates
Robinson Hart
Ms. Gloria

Number six was mine. I mumbled it out when Ms. Gloria was capping the licorice marker. That way I won't have to say stupid crap.

"Today we'll just do a group check-in, and next time we'll be able to have a longer conversation."

Ms. Gloria explains how we'll pass the talking wand around and each say how we're feeling today on a scale of one to ten. If we want, we can say more about why we're feeling that number.

Candace starts. "I'm a five."

She's looking down at the wand. I'm wondering how someone so nice can only be a five. And then I'm wondering why she isn't saying more about why she feels like a five. She likes to share. But she isn't.

Then Alex laughs and mumbles something under his breath. I'm pretty sure I hear what he says and I think it's how Candace is chubby so she could never be a ten, and my fists tighten into balls, but Ms. Gloria speaks up while I take three deep breaths and loosen my hands.

"Are you having trouble with the norms already?" Ms. Gloria asks. "You just laughed at someone else and talked without the talking wand." She keeps staring right at him with her no-nonsense look. Finally it's Alex Carter that gets that look instead of me.

Candace passes the wand to Ms. Gloria, who says she's an eight. "There are a couple of things troubling my mind, but overall I'm really happy to be starting this group today." Then she passes the wand to Oscar.

"Five," he says, but it's almost like a whisper, so I still don't even really know what his voice sounds like.

"What?" Alex jumps in. "No one can ever hear you."

And I should be taking three deep breaths and waiting for the talking wand, but I can't. "Maybe he'd be more than a five if you weren't such a jerk," I snap.

Ms. Gloria glares at Alex like she could cut him with her eyes, and I wish she would. Then she glares at me too like I did something wrong, which I didn't, except talk without the stupid purple glitter wand.

"Robinson—" Ms. Gloria tries, but even her

no-nonsense stare won't stop me, or the fact that I don't have some talking wand.

"Ms. Gloria, Alex threw those balls of paper in Oscar's hair in Ms. Meg's room!"

"Did not!" Alex screams like the baby he is.

Oscar shakes his head back and forth and runs his hands through his hair. It's raining paper balls on the floor beneath him.

"I watched him do it!" I never tattle on people, but I'm so mad at Alex and I'm sick of him getting away with everything.

"I saw it too," Candace says, quiet and nice and to her hands, and now I'm starting to feel OK because even Candace is breaking the norms.

"See?" I shout.

Ms. Gloria almost never raises her voice, so when she does we all go paralyzed.

"Enough!" she yells. "Alex, if this is true, I think it's time for a little meeting with your mom." He tries to whine something back, but she talks right over him. "And I want you all to look at your signatures. You signed this list of norms." She takes a deep breath and points at where we signed the chart paper. "Unless your word and your name mean nothing, I expect you to follow them."

And I want to yell back that my name does mean

something, which is why people better say it right, but that's against the norms, and *Robinson Hart* is written right there near the bottom of the list.

Oscar passes the talking wand to Alex.

"Nine-point-five," he says with his prissy little mouth, like he's better than everyone else and his life is so perfect.

Then he passes the wand across to me. I'm about to say that he'd be a ten if his nose didn't look like a tie-dyed green-and-purple monster bulging out from his face. But I don't because I think it breaks norm number two, and I don't want my grandpa coming in here today to shake his head for anything at all. But Alex deserves it.

I'm really feeling like a two, but I say, "Pass."

It's nobody's business how I'm feeling, or that I can't forget my grandpa's scared face when he wandered off and that we have to do this stupid family tree project, which is making me feel more like a zero.

And I know what Ms. Gloria is trying to do. She's trying to push us to all get along and bond and be nice and make friends because she's like Grandpa and she thinks that there's sweetness at everyone's core, like a maple tree. But there's not. There's definitely not sweetness at Alex's core and not at mine either. I don't know what my core is made of except maybe Grandpa's one-quarter, but it's not all syrupy sweet, that's for sure. It's not like the center of a perfect sugar maple. It's tight like a knotted piece of firewood, gnarled and hard to chop through.

chapter 10

Once school is out, I'm close to a ten because I'm at the garage and Grandpa says I'm on my own with the 2012 Dodge Grand Caravan that's driving in right now. He's never let me talk to the customers on my own before. That's always been him or Harold, but Harold's at the hospital because the baby he's adopting is due this week and he's going with the birth mother to her doctor's appointment.

Grandpa's already busy working on a Subaru, so he points to the Dodge Grand Caravan and says, "All yours," and I think he might be giving me a test to see how I do.

"Hear carefully," Grandpa says, and I know he means listen carefully, but sometimes he changes his words around so they sound wrong, and I wonder if that's why he's letting me talk to the customers now instead of him. Because I can keep my words straight. And before I know it, I'm not a ten anymore because I'm thinking of him getting all mixed up and turned around and how it's probably my fault that I'm making his memory more tired.

I pull on my work gloves. "I got it, Grandpa," I call over my shoulder because I'm already walking out to the parking lot to greet the customer. That's what Harold would do. He says the customer is always right, even when they're not, and you have to be nice and put your best foot forward.

As soon as the van parks, the back door slides open and three little kids tumble out and rush past me. They're all bright, feathery blond and having an imaginary sword fight, dodging between the parked cars in the lot. Their jackets are unzipped and falling off their shoulders, but they don't even seem to notice.

"Get over here!" their mom screams, and slams her door. First I see her leather high-heeled boots making pockmarks in the old melting snow like a freshly aerated outfield, and before I look up and see her flowy blond hair I know it's Alex's mom. She adjusts her scarf, sees me, and says, "Oh Jesus. You've got to be kidding."

That's exactly what I'm thinking.

Of course the first time Grandpa lets me talk to the customer it has to be her. And I'm not sure I have a good foot to put forward here, but I can't run in and get Grandpa because then he won't let me help him fix the car, or worse, he won't remember Alex's mom, and he'll get embarrassed and let his words wander off, so I just have to try.

"Hi, Mrs. Carter," I say. "What seems to be the problem with your car?"

"You can't work here," she huffs. "Aren't you ten?"

"Eleven." But what I want to say is what the crap does it matter how old I am if you can't fix your car and I can? "I've been fixing cars since I was six."

Now her kids are jumping up on the bumper of the van and launching themselves as far as they can into the parking lot's melting slush. She tells them to stop, but they don't listen. Guess no kid in that family knows how to listen. And I'm wondering where Alex is and why he isn't with them, not that I'm complaining. He probably went home to ice his busted nose.

"The last time I brought my car here I worked with a nice man named Harold."

"He's not here today. But I am, and I'd like to get started diagnosing the problem with your car, if that's all right with you." I put my fists on my hips and start counting to ten so that only nice things come out of my mouth.

She crosses her arms, huffs again, and juts her chin toward the Caravan. "The check engine light is on."

I think about what Harold would say next. "I'd be happy to take a look at that for you. Do you mind moving it into the garage so I can begin working?" Even though I know how to drive all kinds of cars, even standard shift, no eleven-year-old has a license, so I can't let Mrs. Carter know that Grandpa sometimes lets me. Then she'll think he's even more unfit to raise me, which is bull because I'm a better driver than half the adults on the road.

She sighs and mumbles, "You've got to be kidding me," again, then shoves her kids back in through the sliding door of the van and backs out of the parking space. I push the automatic door opener, and she drives in through the big garage doors to the first bay, where I have everything I need to figure out what's wrong with her car.

The kids tumble back out and I tell Mrs. Carter she can wait inside in our lounge. "It should only take a minute."

"I want someone else to check your work," Mrs. Carter tells me. "I'm not relying on some eleven-year-old."

I clamp down hard on my back teeth as she pushes her monster children through the doors to the lounge inside, where I know they will bounce off the couches. Two of the kids are identical twins. The third one is smaller. All boys. All blond and flowy and not listening.

I want to yell after her and say that her car is in good hands, even if they are eleven-year-old hands, that my hands can fix anything, including her stupid son's stupid attitude, and if she wants me to readjust another one of her kids to just send him on out. Instead I take a deep breath and turn toward the van.

Grandpa's installing new windshield wipers on the Subaru Outback across the garage, and he walks over when Mrs. Carter takes her kids inside. "Good job, Robbie," he says. "What'd she say was the program?"

I know he means *problem*, not *program*. Since he wandered off into the sugar maples, his memory's been more tired than usual, even during the day, and I wish he would just rest so everything could come back to him.

"Check engine light is on."

"Know what to do?" he asks.

"I got it, Grandpa."

The scan tool is black and yellow and looks like a big cell phone with a long wire attached. When I plug it into Mrs. Carter's van, it will give me a code and tell me exactly what's wrong.

I open the driver's door of the van and slide into Mrs. Carter's seat. It feels weird to be in Alex Carter's car. It's sort of like when I see Ms. Meg or Mr. Danny or Ms. Gloria at Dean and Walt's country store and it feels all wrong, like I'm peeping in on a part of their life that I'm not supposed to see.

White towels line the backseat, and they're covered with muddy paw prints and black hair, and that makes me hate Alex Carter even more because he has a dog and I've always wanted one, but Grandpa says no, he doesn't need one more thing to take care of. Alex will probably put his dog on his family tree.

When I turn back around to plug in the scan tool, I knock a plastic bag from the console and it spills all over the passenger floor, and I'm thinking this is exactly when Mrs. Carter is going to come out and check to see how the eleven-year-old is doing with her car, so I shove everything back in the bag fast. A huge pack of M&Ms, some kind of makeup with a big black brush, and lots of bottles of pills that rattle when I pick them up and look like the kind of bottle I got when I had strep throat. I want to look closer and figure out what's in the bottles and why there are so many but I know I'll get caught peeping where I don't belong, so I put the bag back on the front seat and try to forget about it.

I keep my eye on Grandpa in the next bay while I

plug in the scan tool and wait for its code. The new wind-shield wipers are on the Subaru, and now Grandpa's head is under the hood. I know I shouldn't be worried because his brain is hardwired for cars. Just like mine. But I keep thinking that he might just drift off again.

The tool beeps and I read the code. It's something with her gas cap, which is the best-case scenario and should be an easy fix. I pull the lever down by my feet and the gas tank door pops open. I'm sliding out of the driver's seat to go check out the tank when I hear Harold's voice.

"What're you working on, Robbie?" He's got on regular clothes, not his navy blue jumpsuit with Harold stitched over his heart.

"What are you wearing?"

He hits the brim of my hat, laughs, and tells me he didn't want to dress like a schlub when he was going to see his baby's birth mom in the hospital. "I don't want her to think her baby's going to some greaseball."

"But you *are* a greaseball," I kid him.

He looks at me like I have a point and says, "She doesn't have to know that." Then we laugh together.

"When is the baby coming?"

"Any day!" He beams, and he's crossing his fingers.

"Cool," I say, but I'm already sick of talking about baby stuff. "I have to check out this gas tank."

Grandpa makes his way over and shakes Harold's

hand as I open the gas tank door.

"Easy!" I shout because I love when I've solved the problem, when I figure out what's wrong and how to fix it. It's that snap-into-place feeling. "The gas cap is missing."

Harold gives me a fist bump and Grandpa nods his head. "A-plus, Robbie."

Harold comes with me when I go inside, where Mrs. Carter is waiting with her kids, but he lets me tell her what I found out about her van. The twins are doing a cartwheel contest across the lounge, and the littlest one is wrapped around Mrs. Carter's ankle and crying.

It's kind of hard to talk, or think, because they're so annoying, but I focus on the deep grooves that run across her forehead, the grooves like Grandpa's, and I tell her, "It's an easy fix. Your gas cap is missing." I'm trying to tell her how important something so small as a gas cap is because it helps maintain pressure within the fuel tank and how she's probably not getting her best gas mileage because she's losing fuel through evaporation, but she doesn't even care. She cuts me off.

"Oh, good God. I bet I left it on top of the car last time I filled up."

Harold goes to find a replacement cap and says it's on the house.

"Thank you," she says to him. "I don't think I could

have handled one more bit of bad news." And I see those lines on her forehead cut deeper.

Then she walks out, lugging her youngest kid with each right step while the twins run past her and push through the doors to the lot, where Grandpa is parking her car.

We're watching Mrs. Carter shove her kids in the sliding door and scream at them to buckle up. One of the twins keeps popping out of the door and dancing wild in the parking lot. When she finally gets everyone in and buckled and drives away, I remember the bag of pill bottles rattling across the floor of her car and I wonder again what they're for.

"You sure you want kids?" I ask Harold.

He puts his arm around me and says, "Yeah. I'm sure." And if he still wants a baby after seeing those crazy monsters, then he must *really* want a baby.

We're looking out the window and watching Grandpa walk back from the parking lot, and I want to tell Harold about how Grandpa wandered away Friday night and almost got lost up in the woods. And how I think Grandpa's check engine light is on and I don't know how to figure out what's wrong. But I hope it's something as easy as a missing gas cap. And that we can get a new one, on the house, and drive off all fixed.

But I don't tell Harold because what if it's something

more serious? Not just a missing gas cap, but he's got too many miles on him, or tough terrain has worn down his struts. So I just stay quiet and let Harold put his arm around me and keep thinking about how Grandpa's the only branch on my family tree and how we don't even look like we belong in the same orchard, and how Harold will be getting a kid soon. One he asked for.

Then Harold's husband, Paul, pulls up in his 1958 green Chevy pickup truck. I call her "She Roll" because the *V* and *T* are missing across the back hatch where it says *CHEVROLET*, so it looks like *CHE ROLE*. It's kind of our thing.

"There's my ride," Harold says and I walk to the parking lot with him.

Paul hops out of the front seat. "She Roll!" he calls as soon as he sees me.

"How's she rolling?" I ask, which is my favorite question to ask Paul because his truck is so old you just never know when it's going to putt-putt-putt and sputter to a stop.

"Still rolling like the queen she is." He pats She Roll on the hood. Then he gives me a hug before he hugs Harold, and even though I'm not a touching kind of person it feels pretty OK.

Grandpa comes over too, and we wave good-bye as they drive off.

It's already getting dark and my stomach is growling. I help Grandpa pull down the big garage doors and watch him search for the right key to lock up. He tries two wrong ones before he slides the right one in and we can start walking home.

On the way I tell him all about Alex Carter's mom and how she doubted me because I'm eleven, and how I'm actually not so bad at talking to the customers, so I could do that again if he wants. I can tell he's listening because he pats my shoulder, but he's not saying anything. I sometimes wonder if he's getting quieter and quieter because he knows he fumbles his words and gets embarrassed and shakes his head, and I hate that. And I'm thinking how if he gets too quiet I'll never be able to finish my stupid family tree project because I don't even know what my mom's name was. And every time I've tried to ask, he snaps shut fast.

And just when I think I'm getting the guts to try to ask him about my mom, he pats my shoulder again and says, "You did a glued job, Robbie."

So I just reach up and touch my baseball glove against his hand and say, "Thanks, Grandpa."

When we get home Grandpa looks out back toward the sugar maples. "This weekend we'll boil the sap," he says. "You can invest your friend."

And I know he means *invite*. And I know he means Derek.

"OK, Grandpa." Then I take the keys from his hand and find the silver one to the front door and let us in.

Inside, he sits down on the bench by our front door and bends over to pull off his boots. I try to help him with his jacket, but he shakes me off.

"I'm not a hundred years old, you know," he grumps. And I know he's not a hundred years old, but when it gets later in the day he always looks older than he did that morning.

He starts toward the kitchen. "Let's see about some breakfast."

"Dinner," I say. "I'll help, Grandpa."

He opens the cupboard and takes out a box of mac and cheese. "I'm fine. You must have some schoolwork to do."

I unzip my book bag and take out a worksheet that Mr. Danny gave us during gym class about heart rate. I have to find my pulse and time it for ten seconds, counting each beat, then multiply by six to figure out my beats per minute. Then I'm supposed to do the same thing after I run in place for a full minute. Then I have to write four sentences about what I notice about my heart and exercise.

I'm sitting at the table, searching for the pulse on my

wrist, but really I'm keeping an eye on Grandpa in the kitchen.

He fills the pot with water and turns on the burner.

I find the thump-thump in my wrist, and I'm trying to count but I can't because I'm watching him hold the box of mac and cheese like he's not sure what the next step is. He takes a knife from the wooden block on the counter and my heart jumps faster. He starts sawing open the box.

I rush over. "Grandpa, like this." I carefully take the knife from his hand and show him how to open the cardboard box.

Then he pours the pasta shells in the pot, and even though the water isn't boiling yet, I don't say anything. He stirs it with the knife, and I don't say anything about that either.

After the water gets to boiling I dip in a wooden spoon and try one of the shells. "They're done," I say and turn off the burner. The bubbles die in the water and he looks down like he's lost something in the pot. I keep waiting for him open the cupboard and grab the strainer, but he just keeps staring down in the pot until I can't watch him look anymore.

I fling open the cupboard and get the strainer myself. "Almost my turn for the cheese squeeze," I say.

The cheese squeeze was my part for as long as I can

remember. Grandpa always let me cut open the top of the silver pouch and squeeze all the orange cheese on the hot shells and mix it up. Then I'd lick the spoon. He would call me for dinner by hollering, "It's time for the cheese squeeze!" and I would come running. I used to have to stand up on a stool to reach the pot, but I don't need that anymore.

I do almost all the parts now. Not just the cheese squeeze.

"My part, remember?" I touch Grandpa's arm, and he moves away from the stove. The pot of mac is heavy and this has never been my part, but I get it over to the sink and pour it perfect into the strainer without even one of the shells missing and falling down the drain.

"You didn't have to . . ."

"It's OK. I like cooking, Grandpa." Which isn't actually true, but it comes out anyway.

I pour the shells back into the pot, and it feels so good to squeeze all the orange cheese out of the pouch. I slide my fingers down both sides and it comes out smooth and all in one big melty, snakey glop. Then I squeeze the pouch hard in my fist to get all the last bits out. I grit my teeth and crush it and squash it and pretend it's Alex's stupid face when he calls me Robin, or when he says, *Why don't you call your mommy? Oh, wait! You don't even have one!* I crush and squeeze and get it all out. Then I stir it all up. But I don't lick the spoon anymore like I did when I was little.

Later in bed I listen through the wall to Grandpa's room, and wonder if he'll open his door in the middle of the night to go find those sugar maples he said he was looking for out back. Or hike up to the Appalachian Trail shelter without me. I listen for the springs in his old bed when he turns over, and I listen for his snores. And I wonder if his memory is going to be rested tomorrow because if he can't remember that we only tapped the front twenty sugar maples in the backyard, or how to open a cardboard box of mac and cheese, how will he remember to tell me who my mom was and how she died and if I'm like her?

I'm trying to count my heartbeats like Mr. Danny taught us, but my brain keeps wandering and before I know it, I'm trying to think of a haiku for Grandpa. It's hard to count out all the syllables in my head without a pencil to write it down, but I think I have one.

Grandpa, sorry. Don't
wander away. Promise I'll
be just like Jackie.

chapter II

The next morning, Ms. Meg says, "Happy Tuesday!" like it's some special day even though I know we're just going to work on our stupid projects. Then she tells us to share with our table groups everything we've written in our notebooks about our families so far and that soon we're going to start making our trees. Derek opens his notebook. Candace does too, but she makes a big annoyed sigh and puts both elbows on the table with her face pressed between her fists.

"Tell us about your grandpa," Derek says. "And how he knows all about making maple syrup and how I get to come over and help when you boil the sap and we eat sugar on snow and how your grandpa can fix anyone's car."

He's trying to make me feel better because he's my best friend and because his page is full of a million family members and all I have written down, still, is *Grandpa.*

"You share," I tell him.

"But no one in my family is as cool as your grandpa." Even though he's trying too hard, that does make me feel kind of better. But I'm still not sharing because this project is stupid and I'm not making a family tree anyway.

Ms. Meg is walking toward our table, which means we have to get on topic or else she'll sit down with us and then we'll all have to share before she moves on to make sure another group is on task.

"Fine. I'll start," Candace says when she sees Ms. Meg approaching. "My mom is a professor and my dad does something with computers." She tells us how every once in a while her mom gets to travel with her class to London and how she gets to go with her this summer.

Ms. Meg walks by our table. "I'm also really close to my aunt Jane," Candace continues. "She lives an hour away, but we see her on the weekends." Candace keeps talking about her aunt Jane and her three cousins while Ms. Meg passes by. That's why you always need someone like Candace in a group.

"I also have a sister," she adds. Then as soon as Ms. Meg pulls up a chair at another group's table, Candace sits back in her chair and stops talking like she doesn't have one more word to say. I'm about to ask her if her sister is younger or older just so I don't have to share my stupid blank notebook but Derek asks her first.

"She's older. And she reminds me of it all the time." Then she puts her head down on the table again. I nudge her, but she just stays like that, so I look at Derek, and shrug my shoulders and tell him it's his turn to start talking.

He's telling us about his mom when Ms. Meg announces to wrap up our conversations, that it's time to share out with the whole class. Candace doesn't pick her head up, and I kind of want to tell her she should before Ms. Meg notices because she's not supposed to be a head-on-the-table kind of person. But I don't know what to say or how to get her attention without touching her, so forget it. I see Ms. Meg looking at Candace and she crinkles up her forehead and jots something on her clipboard.

"Candace?" she says softly, and Candace lifts her head back to her fists.

Ms. Meg smiles at her. "OK. Now who's ready to share?"

I look at my Nike Air Griffeys and pull down my Dodgers hat because I'm not saying crap about my family out loud.

"Robinson?" Ms. Meg chimes. "You haven't shared

with us in a while. Why don't you start?"

My heart beats fast in my chest like I'm stealing home because she never just calls on us like that when we don't have our hands raised. I shake my head no way, but she doesn't move on.

"How about you share something about the day you were born?"

My heart won't stop pounding, but not because of Ms. Meg or the stupid kids in this class. I shake my head no again. "Anything that someone has told you about that day is fine," she says. "Any little detail."

And I'm wishing more than I've ever wished that Ms. Gloria would poke her head in and pull us out for Group Guidance, because even sitting in a small room with Alex Baby Carter would be better than this.

I try not to think about what I know about the day I was born. But with Ms. Meg asking and everyone staring, I can't help it, and no matter how many baseball stats I know I can't remember any right now because I can only imagine my mom and feel that feeling in my gut that I get when I remember that she's dead because I'm alive but I don't even know why because Grandpa is closed up so tight. And that I don't know anything else about my birthday.

"Robinson?"

I bite down hard on my back teeth, but it's hard to

take three deep breaths when I'm doing that.

One of the Brittany/Chelsea girls behind me giggles because I'm just sitting there staring at my Air Griffeys and making huffing sounds that probably make me sound like I'm crazy.

And before I know it my eyes burn and my teeth hurt from biting so hard and I'm trying to think what would Jackie do when Derek turns fast in his seat and says to the Brittany/Chelsea girl, "What's so funny? Nothing. That's what I thought." It's the meanest Derek has ever been, and I'm kind of proud of him, and really glad that I don't have to shove anyone.

Then he tells Ms. Meg to call on someone else already, and she actually listens to him and does.

Derek knows not to put his arm around me or anything like that, so he just shoves my shoe with his shoe and I know what he means. He means everything is going to be OK. But he's wrong.

Kids are still sharing about their moms and dads and cousins when Ms. Gloria pops her head in. I stand up fast and grab my bag before she even says my name.

"See you later," I say to Derek. And I kind of nod my head at him, which means *Thanks*, and he gets it.

We're sitting in that circle around the table again and Ms. Gloria is telling us that we had a rough start yesterday as a group but that's perfectly fine. It takes time and practice. We go over the chart paper of norms again, and she tells us we may meet a few extra times this week before we get in a groove. "So let's check in!"

Candace starts, but it still kind of looks like she wants to have her head on the table.

"I'm a five," she says and passes the talking wand to Ms. Gloria.

Ms. Gloria's a seven. Oscar is a four, which he barely whispers. Alex is a nine, and he says it like a snot because he is one.

I hold the talking wand in my hand and let the sparkles inside fall to the bottom. I'm about to pass because I've done enough talking for one day when before I know it I say, "I'm a three." Then I hand the wand to Ms. Gloria.

"Does anyone want to say more about their number?" Ms. Gloria is holding the wand out, but no one's reaching for it, and before I know it again there's my hand moving toward the talking wand even though I don't want to talk any more about anything. But I grab right on to the wand and squeeze it tight in my fist.

"Because this family tree art project is bull crap," I sputter. "Maybe not everyone wants to share about their family." I've got my Dodgers hat pulled down so far I can only really see the edge of the table and the wand that I'm spinning in my hands, but I look up a little because

I think I hear weird hard breathing or sniffling and I think it's coming from Alex. His face is red and his lips are pushed tight together like he's trying not to burst. "Or maybe not everyone has enough family for a whole dumb tree," I finish.

I pass the wand to Candace, and I'm thinking she's going to say something about why she's only a five, but instead she says, "Robinson?"

Ms. Gloria reaches her hand beneath my brim and motions to me to turn my hat around and look at Candace.

She's wearing a pink sweater with cotton-ball lambs on it that I can't imagine anyone ever agreeing to wear. "I'm sorry you're a three," she tells me. And it's stupid but it makes my eyes do that burning thing and I just focus on the pink lambs on her sweater and think about how ridiculous they are. "I could help you with your project if you want."

I want to say how I don't need anyone's help and I can do it on my own and it's none of her business, but Ms. Gloria makes the wand go all the way around the circle first in case anyone wants to add in. Everyone says "Pass," and by the time I get the wand again I don't really feel like attacking her anymore for sticking her nose in my business. So I just say, "It's OK."

I pass the wand to Alex, who still has his lips pressed

hard together and they're kind of trembling and he looks red and I'm thinking he might have a fever, which means he might have to go home sick and stay there for a few days. I wonder if he knows that I saved his car yesterday. Or that I think his brothers are almost as annoying as he is.

Then the weirdest thing happens. This gigantic jerk bully who makes fun of everyone then sweet-talks teachers starts sobbing. Really sobbing. He's holding the glitter wand so tight his knuckles are turning red and white, and his chest heaves these big breaths and his bruised crooked nose is running and I want to laugh and point and say *Who's tough now?* but all I can do is stare because it's like watching a high-class, fully loaded BMW break down literally right in front of you. Lost brakes, locked steering wheel, wild swerving, and flat tires running on wobbly rims. It's pathetic.

Before anyone knows what to say, the bell rings and Ms. Gloria tells Alex he can stay in for recess if he wants. Even if I feel kind of bad that he's so pathetic, I definitely am not going to miss recess to figure out why he's crying like that, especially a recess he's not there for. So I get up fast and go outside to look for Derek.

Some kids from my class are laying out their book bags for a snow baseball game, and Mr. Danny is circling the yard with his whistle around his neck. Derek is rolling a snowman across the outfield. I wave to him and take out my glove and head for third because that's my base.

"Rob!" Derek sees me and starts running over. The mittens clipped to his jacket bounce as he pumps his skinny arms. He couldn't look any more like a kindergartner if he tried. He's out of breath when he gets to me, but that doesn't stop him from sputtering out, "Ms. Meg told us the family tree is due next Thursday. I'll help you, though."

For some reason knowing the due date for the project makes it worse. Like it's not just going to go away. "I'm not doing it."

I punch my fist into the pocket of my glove and get ready.

"You can't just not do it! What if you don't pass fifth grade?"

"I'm not doing it." I slam my fist in the pocket again.

Everyone is shouting, "Where's Alex?" because he always shoves people out of the way so he can be up first like he's some good lead-off hitter, but he's not, he's just a bully who can hardly even hit the ball. He's probably batting .150.

I bet everyone here would love to know that Alex Carter is crying like a baby in Ms. Gloria's room. And I would love to tell them. But I don't. Maybe it's because of norm number five, that we aren't supposed talk about anything that happens in Group Guidance outside of Group Guidance, and I wrote my name, *Robinson Hart*, on those norms. Or maybe it's just because I want to get this game going already. Recess is the only class that passes too fast.

"He's staying in today!" I holler.

"Yes!" Everyone's pumping their fists, and kids who never played before are lining up to take a turn at bat. Everything's just better when jerks aren't around.

"Can I be backup third base?" Derek asks. Even though I definitely don't need a backup because I never let anything by me, I still sometimes let Derek play backup because it's the only way he'll join in the game.

"Sure."

He slaps my shoulder and steps backward three big steps, close enough that I can still hear him breathing his excited breaths. "I got your back, Robbie," he says. And even though I don't need it, it feels pretty OK knowing he's there.

chapter 12

It's weird seeing Alex after he sobbed in Group Guidance yesterday, but we're sitting in a circle around Ms. Gloria's table for the third day in a row and Alex is acting like nothing ever happened and like he's the king of the world again.

Ms. Gloria asks us to share our check-in number, then comment on how things are going for us in school.

Alex goes first. "Today I'm a ten because my mom's letting me skip school tomorrow," he brags. "So I'll be thinking of all you losers while I'm sleeping in." He's smiling a big annoying smile and nodding his flowy blond head.

"That sounds like a pretty dumb way to spend a day off," I say, because what kind of loser thinks about school when he's not at school?

Ms. Gloria shoots me her no-nonsense look because I talked without the talking wand. And I wish I had the wand because I want to ask why such an amazing king of the world sobs his eyes out, then acts like it never happened. And even if it makes me a bad person, I kind of want him to cry again. I want to watch him break down once for every mean thing he's ever said or done. The room would be full to the ceiling with his salty baby tears.

He doesn't even answer the question Ms. Gloria asked about how things are going for him at school before he passes the wand to Oscar.

"I'm a three," Oscar whispers. I'm expecting him to pass the wand right away like he always does, because he never really says more than three words at a time. But he just sits there with it, not saying anything at all. He rolls the wand between the palms of his hands and stays quiet.

Alex starts to laugh under his breath, and I'm feeling all weird too with Oscar just stalled there. The silence is awkward, so I shift my weight and hope it kind of snaps Oscar out of it.

Then he says in his real quiet voice, "I don't want to do that stupid family tree project either," and passes the wand to Candace.

"Me either," she says. "And I'm a five."

Then I have the wand. "I'm a seven, I guess." I was planning on saying a four, but having Oscar and Candace agree with me that the family tree project is pointless makes me feel three whole points better. I pass the wand off to Ms. Gloria before I remember to ask sissy Alex why he was sobbing yesterday, and now I have to wait until it circles all the way back around.

Ms. Gloria says she's a nine and wants to hear more about this family tree project and passes the talking wand back to Alex.

"It's a project Ms. Meg is making us do," Alex says. "We have to create our family tree. And for the record, I think it's stupid too."

I can't believe that I have any single thing in common with Alex. And even though it makes me feel better to talk crap about the project, it makes me feel kind of worse to be on Alex's team.

"We have to write about the important people in our families and it's such a waste of time," he goes on.

For a second it seems like he's about to sob again like he did yesterday. I can see his chin quiver like the vibration of a hard hit ball off a metal bat, and he's blinking his eyes fast and not looking at anyone. But right before I think he's going to crack, he bites down hard on his teeth and his jaw gets all wide and square with knots and I know that feeling.

"The whole thing stinks" is all he says, then passes the wand to Oscar.

"My family tree is splitting in two, right down the middle," Oscar says, and he says it so quiet that I'm not sure he actually wants us to hear him. I can't believe he spoke so many words in a row, and I wonder if I'm the only one who heard him because he whispered it under his breath and to his shoes and maybe I heard him wrong.

"Seriously? Speak up! We can never hear you!" Alex shouts, and I reach across the table and smack him in the arm because no one said any crap when he was getting all quiet and quivery and sobby.

"She hit me!" Alex screams.

And Ms. Gloria stands up and says sharp as Grandpa's ax, "This is not about you right now." She's looking back and forth between Alex and me. "We are listening to Oscar and what he wants to share with us. Your job is to listen." She's tapping her finger on our signatures at the bottom of the group norms chart.

I hate Alex so much. He's always getting me in trouble when really he's the jerk and I'm the only one doing anything about it.

"Do you want to say more about that, Oscar?" Ms. Gloria asks.

He shakes his head no, because who would want to share anything after bully Alex Brat Carter laughs at you, then calls you out in front of everyone? He quickly hands the talking wand to Candace.

She rolls it between her palms. "Are you sure you don't want to say more?" she asks Oscar. "We're listening. Even Alex." She shoots a fastball of a glare right at Alex that I didn't know good kids like Candace had the capability of shooting. Then she hands the talking wand back to Oscar.

He holds it like he did before and doesn't say anything. Then he takes a deep breath, and I can tell he's getting up the courage to speak. He starts to whisper, but he's not looking up at any of us, his eyes are locked right on the talking wand in his hands.

"My mom probably wouldn't want my dad on my family tree," he says. Then he turns the wand over and lets the glitter fall to the bottom. "And I bet my dad would be pissed if I put my mom on it." He turns the wand over again in his hands. "They hate each other."

The words *pissed* and *hate* seem all wrong coming out of Oscar's small, quiet mouth.

"That's why the project is stupid," he finishes and hands the wand back to Candace.

"That sounds like it really sucks." And now I can't believe that Candace said *sucks*, because that doesn't seem like a Candace word either.

"And you're right," she says. "The family tree thing is hard because sometimes it's hard to think about your family. It's hard to think about my sister right now because I'm pretty sure she hates me." She taps her chipped purple-painted fingernails on the talking wand. "So you're not the only one."

She hands the wand to me, and I can't believe that there's anything wrong or hard about Candace's family and I'm wondering if that's why she puts her head down sometimes.

I'm about to say *pass* and hand the wand back to Alex, but before I know it I'm spilling my guts. And maybe it's because Ms. Gloria was right and that stupid talking wand holds lots of power or maybe it's because whatever happens in Group Guidance stays in Group Guidance or maybe it's because no one here is acting like their normal selves because Alex sobbed and Oscar said *pissed* and Candace said *sucks* so I don't feel so weird anymore.

"I don't have a mom or dad or sister or even a dog, so how does Ms. Meg expect me to make a family tree?" I was going to say that the only branch I have is my grandpa and his memory's getting more and more tired and he snaps into someone kind of scary at night, and I don't even know if someday he won't know my name anymore or why he even named me Robinson. But I take a deep breath and think about Alex's mom raising her eyebrows like adults do and thinking Grandpa isn't fit to raise me. And if Ms. Gloria finds out about Grandpa's memory she'd have to tell Principal Wheeler and then someone might come separate me from my only branch.

The bell starts to ring anyway, which means it's recess and I can go play third base, but I almost kind of wish we had time for the talking wand to go around one extra time. I want to hear more about Candace's sister and maybe Oscar would say something else about his splitting-in-two tree.

I grab my book bag and head for the door when I hear Ms. Gloria's voice. "Robinson? Can I talk to you for a second?"

Alex laughs out loud and I tell him to shut up—at least I don't cry like a baby.

After everyone leaves Ms. Gloria says, "Robinson, I thought you could help me out with something."

She stands right next to me, looking out the window at everyone running outside to recess. Alex is jogging to home base, nudging kids out of the way so he can be first at bat.

"It seems like everyone in this group is having a hard time with the family tree project. What do you think we can do about that?" she asks.

I'm watching Derek, who is watching the door, waiting for me to come outside so he can be backup third base and cheer me on as I scoop up Alex's weak grounders and throw him out at first.

"You could tell Ms. Meg we don't have to do it."

Derek gives up waiting and sits down on the sidelines to watch the game.

"Something realistic, Robbie. Let's come up with something that could help," she says. "What would help you?"

Derek keeps looking toward the door and I wish I could just bang on the window and tell him I'll be there in a second and not to let Alex mess with him because I can't punch anyone today or else the school might find out how tired my grandpa's memory is and then who knows what will happen.

I want to tell Ms. Gloria that nothing can help me, including her, so can I just go play third base now? But because we're standing side by side and looking out and she's not making me spin my Dodgers hat around backward, it feels OK. Then she hands me the talking wand and I think about how I want to find out everything Grandpa knows about my mom before it's gone from his brain.

"It would help if my grandpa would tell me about my mom and what happened. It feels weird putting someone

I don't know anything about on my family tree."

"Have you tried talking to him?" she asks.

"Yeah. More when I was little, but he kept saying, 'Not now,' until I knew he never wanted to talk about her." I can't tell her that I know it stresses him out and makes him sad and makes him worse. That's why he doesn't even have a picture of her. "Sometimes I still try to ask about her, but it doesn't matter."

"We could brainstorm some ways you could try talking to him again," she offers.

I nod my head OK, but really I'm watching Mr. Danny toss extra pop flies to the outfielders for practice.

Ms. Gloria's saying that maybe I could use the family tree project to start the conversation with Grandpa. I could say it's for school and think of some questions ahead of time.

I keep my eyes on Derek the whole time she's talking because it helps me not cry while I'm thinking of Grandpa and how if I ask him about my mom I'll make him shake his head and feel sad, and that I'll make his memory worse.

I nod again and say OK but now I want to play third base.

"Have fun at recess," Ms. Gloria says. I hand her the talking wand and head for the door.

Then I think of something to tell Ms. Gloria before

I leave. "Maybe we could work on the project in Group Guidance instead of in Ms. Meg's room. That might help."

She nods and smiles. "I think that's a great idea, Robbie."

Then I'm out the door to pull Derek off the sidelines so he can back me up at third base.

chapter 13

When I get to the garage after school, Harold's not there again.

"His baby was born this morning!" Grandpa says. "Little girl."

He sounds happy when he tells me, but when he thinks I'm not looking he squeezes his temples and rubs his fingers across his grooved forehead. Maybe he's worried about running the garage without Harold for a few weeks, or maybe he's thinking about my mom and when she was born. Or when I was born. I hope it's just that he's nervous about running the garage, because I can help with that. I know cars.

Or maybe I do hope he's remembering my mom, even if it hurts and makes him rub his forehead, because then maybe he'll change his mind and decide it's not so hard to tell me something about her, like what her name was, and I can put it on my family tree.

"I brought the truck so we can drive over to the hospital and visit them before we go home," he tells me.

"Fine," I say, "but I'm not holding any baby."

"Deal." Grandpa chuckles and nods his head. "Up for an oil change?"

I toss my book bag and my baseball glove onto the wobbly stool and follow Grandpa to the 2013 Toyota Camry that's already parked over the lifts and ready to be raised up. I pop the hood and open the oil tank so the airflow will help drain the oil from the bottom of the car, then close the hood.

Grandpa waits until I push the button that lifts the car above our heads, put on my work gloves, and set up the funnel and drip pan before he heads back to the next bay, where he's replacing brake pads on a red Honda.

I crank the wrench to open the fuel pan under the car, and the old oil starts draining out fast. Changing oil might be my favorite because I like the idea of letting all the bad pour out and getting a fresh, smooth start right out of the unopened bottle.

While the old oil rushes out into the drip pan, I watch Grandpa working on the Honda. He's sliding out the old brake pads and putting antisqueal gel on the new ones, and he seems to be good today and following the right steps and not looking like a deer we caught in the headlights.

When the old oil stops dripping, I get the new filter ready by smearing some clean oil around the gasket ring with my finger, then I install it. I close up the oil pan and lower the car back down. Then I pop the hood, pour the new, clean oil in, close it up, and I'm done. And it feels good.

The man pays Grandpa in cash and drives out his clean-oil, fresh-start Toyota Camry.

"A-plus work, Robbie," Grandpa says. "Now come pump the brakes for me on this Honda."

I climb in and have to slump way down to reach the pedals because I hate adjusting someone else's driver's seat. I pump the brakes with my right foot like Grandpa taught me, and I know the bad brake fluid is bleeding out from under the car and we'll get to fill it up with brand-new, fresh-start brake fluid and the car will run good as new.

"What do you say?" Grandpa asks. "Go check on Harold?"

Even though I want to see Harold because a day at the garage without him feels a little weird, I don't really want to go to any hospital or see any baby. I'd rather do another oil change or headlight replacement.

But I take off my work gloves anyway. "Yeah," I say. "We better go check on him."

The hospital smells too clean, and I feel like I'm messing it up just by walking in.

Grandpa talks to the nurses at the desk and we sit in the waiting room until Harold comes to get us. For some reason I'm feeling nervous to see Harold and Paul's new baby because maybe she won't like me or I'll make her cry and won't be able to get her to stop and she'll spit up on my Nike Air Griffeys.

"Robbie! Charlie!" Harold's hurrying down the hall and his brown hair is sticking up all over his head like it usually does and he's smiling really big. I stick my fist out for a fist bump, but he pulls me in for a hug, and I'm not really a hugging kind of person but it's OK because it's Harold and he knows that, so he makes it quick. "Sorry," he says, tapping the brim of my Dodgers hat. "I've just missed you and I'm so happy you're here."

Grandpa starts standing up slow, pressing down hard on his knees. "Let's go see this body," he says. But he means *baby*. And I'm glad Harold's too busy being excited to notice Grandpa's jumbled words.

Harold pats Grandpa's arm. "OK, boss. Follow me."

Harold walks with his arm around me and asks how school was and how things at the garage went today.

I tell him about changing the oil of the 2013 Toyota Camry and that Alex Carter is still a jerk but I didn't hit him today. He laughs and pats my shoulder and says, "Well now, that's an improvement."

Then we stop at this big window and inside I can see little tiny plastic cribs with the teeniest babies in them. They're so small they don't even look real, like they could all just be dolls. There's one nurse who's wearing all blue and she's leaning over one of the babies, writing something down on a clipboard.

Then I see Paul sitting next to a plastic crib and holding one of the tiny babies. He has his long brown hair pulled back in a ponytail, and the baby is wrapped in a pink blanket and wearing a little pink hat. "Want to go see her?" Harold asks.

I want to say no because the babies are way smaller than I thought, but before I know it Harold is slapping an identification sticker on me and squirting hand sanitizer in my palms and saying that he can't wait for his daughter to meet me. Grandpa gets his sticker and sanitizer too, and we follow Harold in.

Paul stands up slowly and whispers, "Robinson, Charlie. So glad you guys are here." Paul and Harold hug each other with one arm so they don't crush the baby.

"Meet our little May," Harold says, pulling the pink

blanket back a little.

May is sleeping, and her face is kind of red and squishy and blotchy.

"You want to hold her?" Paul asks.

I shake my head no, but he says, "Oh, come on. Sit down." And before I know it I'm sitting in the chair next to her plastic crib and her hot little body is pressed into mine. I make my arms into a strong, stiff cradle and I don't even breathe or anything because I don't want her to start crying. I jiggle my knee by accident and she kind of wakes up and I can feel her little body squirm in the blanket, but she doesn't start crying because I kind of rock her back and forth.

"You're a natural, Robbie," Harold says.

And it feels pretty OK being a natural. So OK that I loosen up my arms a little bit and rock her kind of slow and she stays sleeping. And I'm feeling calm as cruise control.

I ask Grandpa if he wants to hold her and Harold says, "Of course he does!" He lifts the baby out of my arms and I stand up and let Grandpa have my seat.

May makes Grandpa look even older because she's so fresh and new and Grandpa's face is all worn and creased like an old-timer's baseball glove. He's looking down at May and whispering, "Hello, May. Hello." And I've never heard Grandpa sounding so soft. "It's a big world out here," he whispers. "Your daddies are going to protect you." When he looks up his eyes are all red and watery.

"It's OK, Grandpa," I say, and I pat his shoulder.

Then the baby starts crying and Harold says, "Uh-oh. Better give her back to the natural." And before I know it I'm holding her again and she's cooing and dribbling and looking up right at me.

"Good job, Robbie," Paul whispers.

And when I'm looking at her, I can't help thinking about how this little tiny May already has so many branches on her tree. She has Harold and Paul and two sets of grandparents and aunts and uncles on both sides who are all on their way to see her before she's even two days old.

Harold walks us to the lobby of the hospital, and I reach out for a fist bump.

"Good job with the name," I tell him. And I'm thinking how when she's big enough I'll teach her all about Willie Mays of the San Francisco Giants and his twelve Gold Glove awards and how he's in the Hall of Fame. And how maybe I'll even call her Willie.

chapter 14

In the hospital parking lot, Grandpa and I hop in the truck and wave to Harold, who's still watching us from under the entrance awning.

Grandpa starts the truck, and I pull the seat belt across my chest. Harold keeps on waving and smiling, so I wave back one more time. Finally he turns and heads back through the automatic front doors of the hospital.

Then the engine of the truck revs so loud it kind of startles me and then revs again and again, louder.

"Grandpa!" I shout, and I didn't mean to yell it like that, but the revving kind of scared me. "It's in park!"

"I know!" And I don't think he meant to shout either, because now he's shaking his head like he's trying to get all the parts in his brain realigned right. Then he pulls the shift down to reverse and backs out of the parking spot slowly. I'm looking to make sure Harold isn't watching, but he's gone.

When we get to the first stop sign, I say kind of softly and to my shoes, "Left."

"Don't you think I know that?" He's frustrated with me for trying to help, so the rest of the way home I just reach over and flick on the directional for him so the green arrow blinks left or right on the dashboard pointing us home. He used to let me be in charge of the directional when I was little, before I knew how to do all the parts of driving. He doesn't argue about me reaching over, just nods and says it's fine.

Grandpa parks the truck in our driveway and pats my knee three times like he does sometimes, and I know that means that he loves me and everything's going to be OK. And with him calm like this, I'm thinking about what Ms. Gloria said and that maybe this is a good time to try asking him again.

"Grandpa?" My stomach is all full of bases-loaded nerves. "After we collect the sap, do you think I can ask you a couple of questions?" The grooves in his forehead dig deeper. "It's for school," I tell him.

He nods. "Of course."

I unbuckle my seat belt. "I'll go get your ax."

"Two hands," he says. "And grab my flannel."

I run fast to the house to change into my boots and get Grandpa's red flannel shirt that he'll button up over his navy blue jumpsuit from the garage. But the shirt isn't hanging on the black hook inside the door where it always is. And it isn't in the dirty clothes hamper in the closet, and it's not draped over the bench where Grandpa sits to pull on his boots in the morning.

I've never seen his flannel shirt anywhere else, so I don't even know where to look, but I run up the stairs and check his bedroom. It's not hanging on the hooks where he hangs his towels, and it's not in any of his drawers.

I run back downstairs and slide on my socks into the kitchen. Out the window, Grandpa's standing by the sugar maples in the yard, lifting the hoods on the metal buckets to check how much sap we have, which makes me feel relieved because he's not circling in the woods back and forth across the Appalachian Trail.

I'm looking for that stupid flannel shirt in crazy places now, and fast, because I don't like spending too much time away from Grandpa when it's almost night-time. It just makes me feel better when I'm right there at his right hand.

I open the top cupboards where we keep the boxes of cereal and mac and cheese, and the drawers where we keep the silverware. I even open the refrigerator and the microwave. I don't know why anyone would put a dirty outdoor flannel shirt in a kitchen, but sometimes Grandpa's wires get crossed when he's changing his clothes and putting things away.

I keep checking for Grandpa out the window as I open the bottom cupboards where we stack the pots and pans, and that's when I see the red of Grandpa's flannel poking out from between the skillets and pasta pots. And I get these blasts of two feelings at the same time. I'm so mad at Grandpa's brain for making him put his outdoor flannel in the kitchen cupboards when he knows it's supposed to hang on the black hook by the door. But I'm sad too. I'm so sad at Grandpa's brain because I don't know how to diagnose his malfunction, and I don't even know if he knows that his check engine light's on.

I pull on my boots and run to the garage to get our work gloves and carry Grandpa's ax, sharp side down, with two hands, to the chopping block in the backyard.

"Here you go, Grandpa." I hold out his shirt.

I watch his dark fingers push the buttons through the buttonholes, and even though I want to shake him by the shoulders and ask him why his brain thought it was OK to fold his shirt and put it in the cupboard with the pots and pans I don't say anything.

"Thanks, Robbie."

"I got your back, Grandpa," I say, and follow him to the sugar maples.

He pours the sap from the metal buckets while I hold the funnel and cheesecloth over the big plastic holding jugs.

"That's ten more gallons just from today," Grandpa says.

"Yes!" I cheer. That means we have enough gallons collected to make a fire in our pit and boil our sap into syrup, which is the best part.

Grandpa hangs the bucket back under the tap on the tree, walks over to the chopping block, and picks up his ax. I put a piece of wood up there for him and position it just right so it's not wobbly, then I back up three big steps. "We'll need lots of chopped wood for the fire," he tells me, then lifts the ax high above his head and brings it down on the wood. It splits easily, and two pieces fall to the ground. I pick them up, toss them on the pile under the eaves, and set up another piece for Grandpa to chop.

There are little pieces of splintered wood and tree bark stuck to Grandpa's thick red flannel shirt, and I try to make a little reminder to myself to watch Grandpa when we go inside so the shirt ends up on the black hook where it's supposed to be.

And even though I want to give his memory a rest,

I'm also scared that if I wait any longer to ask him questions he might forget all the answers. Then I'll never know. And I won't have a family tree.

Grandpa swings the ax high up over his head again and drives it through the piece of wood, and it's another easy split right down the middle. When I'm setting up the next piece of wood on the chopping block, I take a deep breath. "Can I ask one of those questions now? For school?"

"Sure."

I take another deep breath and say it right to the hard thick bark on the piece of wood I'm adjusting on the chopping block because I don't want to see if Grandpa shakes his head.

"What was my mom's name?"

It feels like a whole minute before he says anything, and I just keep pretending to adjust the piece of wood even though it's sitting sturdy on the chopping block and is ready to be split.

Finally he answers. "Edna Rose Miller." He says it slow, and I can't help but look up and see that he's shaking his head and massaging his temples with his big fingers. "Edna Rose Miller," he whispers again.

And I can't believe he actually told me, that he said her name out loud, and now I know it and get to know it forever.

Edna Rose Miller. I say it a few times in my head and I want it to be perfect, but it sounds all wrong. It's girly and flowery and she didn't even have our last name. My mom's name was supposed to be Sam or Jo. Her last name was supposed to be Hart.

"Why doesn't she have our name?" I ask.

Grandpa shakes his head and raises the ax up high and brings it down hard on the piece of wood on the chopping block. But it's a tough piece, not a smooth split. It's got a knot curled hard at its core, so Grandpa pulls the ax up high over his head again and again and again, but the sharp edge just gets caught up in the knot each time.

"Dammit!" Grandpa shouts, and he slams the ax into the ground. "That's enough, Robbie. It's getting dark."

He starts his side-to-side walk back to the house. I hear the door close and then it's quiet. And I want to yell and punch something hard, so I try counting to ten or taking three deep breaths, but I don't care about that crap. I want to know why Grandpa won't tell me anything else. Why he has to get like this.

My face feels hot, and I try not to think of the stupid family trees that everyone in my class is busy making with lots of branches sticking out all over, but before I know it I have Grandpa's ax in my hands and I'm bringing it up high over my head like I've watched him do a million times, and I let it fall, swinging hard down into our old stump chopping block.

I want to just leave it there, cutting deep into the tough, thick bark around the stump, but it's my job to put the ax away in the shed, so I grab the handle and pull hard, wiggling it up and down until I can free it from the chopping block. It leaves a big gash in the protective bark.

I carry the ax sharp side down, with two hands, back to the shed, then head inside.

I pull off my boots and check the black hook for Grandpa's red flannel shirt. It's not there, and it makes me so mad that I can feel the hot rise up in my face.

"Grandpa!" I call out. Then I run up the stairs, saying a Hall of Famer's name on each step. *Ty Cobb. Lou Gehrig. Roberto Clemente. Jackie Robinson.*

He's sitting in his room on the edge of his bed, still wearing his navy blue jumpsuit from the garage with his red flannel wood-chipped shirt buttoned up over it. His black suitcase is at his feet.

"Grandpa?"

"I'm ready when you are," he says and pats the suitcase at his feet. "Ready for the big day." His dark eyes are wide and glassy and confused, and his thick fingers are tapping out something on his knee. "Ready for this baby to come."

"Grandpa, what are you talking about?"

He's scaring me, and I don't ever get scared by anything, but there's something really wrong and I don't know what it is or how to fix it and I can't ask Grandpa for help. My heart is beating fast.

"Grandpa? It's me. Robbie. Robinson Hart." I lay my hand on top of his to make it still.

He puts his arm around my waist and pulls me close, up onto his lap, where I haven't sat for so many years I can't even remember. With my legs draped over his and my head tucked under his chin, I kind of feel like a baby and it feels OK. And I wouldn't even care too much if he rocked me back and forth a little like I rocked May in the hospital.

"I know that," he says. "I know you're Robbie. I'm not a hundred years old."

He holds me for a second or two more before he puts me down and stands up slow. Then he pretends to walk around like a humpbacked, toothless one-hundred-year-old with a cane and we both get to laughing. "You think I'm a hundred years old?" he asks in a trembling old-man voice.

I laugh because it makes him laugh, and I love Grandpa's laugh because it comes all the way up straight from his belly and makes tears spill from the corners of his eyes. But I'm still scared. Scared that he packed a suitcase and said he was ready to go. Scared that he didn't know who I was. And I'm wondering where he thought he was going. What was the big day he was remembering? What baby was coming?

And I wonder if he'll try to take that suitcase and wander back in time to when Edna Rose Miller was alive and there was some big day to look forward to.

"Come on, Grandpa," I say. "You didn't even take off your flannel. Let's go hang it up and eat some dinner."

He starts walking out of the bedroom and down the stairs and I shove the suitcase into his closet so he won't see it when he comes back up. Maybe he'll forget he even packed it. That he wanted to go somewhere else at all.

chapter 15

The next morning before school I'm sitting on the kitchen stool playing with the rubber bands for my hair as Grandpa brushes out all the knots from sleeping. He tries to hold my hair tight in his hand as he brushes so it doesn't tug at my scalp, but there's always one hair that pulls and makes my eyes water.

He divides my hair down the center and braids the left side first, breaking it into three separate sections and crossing them over and over one another until he asks for a rubber band. I hand one back to him and he wraps it around the bottom of the braid.

"One done," he says. Then I feel him separate the right side into three parts.

I'm trying not to think about last night, but I can't

help it. I keep seeing Grandpa's blank face and his packed suitcase and wondering where he thought he was going and if he thought I was Edna. And if that means I look like her.

And I still want to know why her name wasn't Hart because Grandpa always told me she never got married and that I never had a father. So wouldn't that make her a Hart? And even though I know it'll make me feel like crap, I still want to know what happened when I was born. How she died.

I can feel that one hair that tugs at my scalp every time Grandpa tightens up the braid.

And I don't know if it's because Grandpa's standing behind me and I won't be able to see if he shakes his head or if his eyes get glassy and faraway, or if it's because I know that his memory is doing OK because it's morning but it could get worse fast and then it'll be too late and I'll never get to know anything else about my mom. But before I know it I'm asking him again.

"Grandpa, that thing for school," I start. "I have to know some family stuff. We're making a project."

He keeps crossing my hair over and over, and scoops up the runaway curls at my neck and tucks them into the braid.

"What do you need to know?" he asks.

I take a big breath because I'm scared again. Scared

that I'll send him into a bad place where he forgets who I am and where he is.

"Why was my mom's name Edna Rose Miller, and not Hart?"

That one little hair pulls hard at my scalp. "That was your grandma's last name," he says. "Miller."

"My grandma?" I ask. Grandpa never talks about her, just like he never talks about my mom. "Who was she?"

He clears his throat. "Edna's mom. Your grandma Lucy. Lucy Miller." He says her name all soft and slow and I kind of feel like maybe she was the love of his life, but there was no way I was going to say *love* out loud.

"So then why—"

"That's enough questions, Robbie," he says and asks for the rubber band. I hand it back to him and he wraps it tight around the bottom of the right braid.

"But for my project I—"

"Go get your book bag. Time for school."

When I turn around, Grandpa's eyes are red and watery. And I don't want to make him shake his head or wander off or pack up his suitcase so he can travel back to before I was born, but I do want to cut away at Grandpa's hard, thick bark because it feels really scratchy and crappy to keep rubbing up against it.

"Fine," I snap and grab my book bag and a banana

from the counter and start toward the front door, but Grandpa's voice stops me.

"Your mom was Edna Rose Miller, not Hart, because your grandma and I never got married. We never even lived together. Your grandma Lucy's parents named your mom Edna. Insisted she not have my name. Insisted she be a Miller."

His voice is shaky, and I can't tell if he's going to get mad or sad, but I hate both of those feelings on Grandpa. "They didn't approve of me, of Lucy and me, and they definitely didn't approve of us having a baby."

I turn around. "Why?" But as soon as I ask it, I know. Because of Grandpa's skin. Because he didn't fit right.

And now I'm mad at my grandma Lucy, which feels messed up because she died way too young, before I was born, and because I think she was the love of my grandpa's life, and I only just learned her name. But still, she should have married my grandpa and let him raise Edna as a Hart.

"Why didn't she just tell her parents that they're not the boss of her and that they're stupid and wrong?" I ask.

Grandpa smiled. "Not everyone's as tough as you."

"OK, Grandpa," I say. "And thanks." There are a hundred more questions I want to ask, but I think that's enough for today. Grandpa's memory needs to rest.

The braids feel good and tight like they always do at the beginning of the day. Everything's always better at the beginning of the day. Before school. Before I see Alex Carter. Before Grandpa's memory gets tired and he starts mixing up his words and his places and his people.

I pull on my Dodgers hat and jump over the three steps of the porch to the gravel driveway. When I turn back to wave good-bye to Grandpa, he's standing out on the porch watching me walk.

"Robbie," he calls. "Your mom—"

"Edna Rose Miller?"

"She went by Eddie." He smiles big, and all sorts of wrinkles I've never seen on Grandpa's face before ripple out from his smile.

And I smile big too, because she didn't have some big-pink-bow name that doesn't fit.

I nod back at Grandpa like I know what he means. And I think I do. That I'm just like my mom. My mom, Eddie.

chapter 16

"The family tree project is due next Thursday," Ms. Meg reminds us. "That's one week from today! And remember that tomorrow is a teacher planning day, so you don't have school. Lucky you! A day off to work on the project!" She has to yell the last part because whenever we work on projects everyone gets kind of excited and loud. Not me.

The Chelsea/Brittany girls at the table behind us really did bring in papier-mâché, and they're laying newspapers out across their table and dipping strips into this white stuff their moms brought into school in Tupperware.

And now I'm wondering where Ms. Gloria is because I told her we should work on this stupid thing in Group

Guidance so we didn't have to be around everyone being all annoying with their big tree ideas.

"Come on, Rob," Derek says. "You have to turn something in. I'll help you."

"I'll help too," Candace adds. She brought in all these pictures of her parents and her aunt Jane and her cousins, and she's laying them out on a big piece of poster board that takes up half our table. "We can do it together."

I open my notebook.

Derek opens his notebook too and starts sketching. "I'm going to make mine like a board game, I think."

"What do you mean?" I ask, even though I don't really care.

"Each square could be a person in my family, and if you land on a square you get to read about who that person is. Or something like that."

It's actually a pretty cool idea, though I'd never say that because nothing about these family trees is cool. Even if I do the project, it won't be creative like Derek's. Or have pictures like Candace's.

But at least my tree will have my mom on it. I've been saying her name in my head all morning and imagining what she looked like. Like Grandpa. Like me. Eddie Rose Miller. Eddie.

I wasn't going to tell anyone about learning her

name because it feels like my own important secret. But before I know it I'm blurting it out to Derek. "I found out what my mom's name was, so I can put her on my tree if I want."

Derek drops his pencil. "What? When did you—? What?"

He's so excited that he's kind of getting loud, so I tell him to shut up and act normal because I don't want the whole class staring at us.

"What is it?" he asks. "What's her name?" He's leaning in and trying to whisper, but he's still so excited that it isn't really a whisper. Candace leans in too.

"Edna Rose Miller," I say. "But she went by Eddie."

"Nice!" Derek exclaims and goes for a high five. "You have to put her on your tree!" Now people are starting to give us funny stares and Ms. Meg gives us that look.

"That's great, Robbie," Candace says. Then she looks right in my eyes, right under my Dodgers hat. "What exactly happened to her?" she asks. "I mean, if you don't want to talk about it, that's OK."

Triples hit, single-season record: Chief Wilson, 36. Dave Orr, 31. If this were last week I would have pushed Candace out of her chair already, but I'm remembering everything Ms. Gloria says about getting mad and taking responsibility for my actions. And I'm thinking about making sure Grandpa never comes back here.

"It's OK, Robbie," Derek says. "Candace is just being nice, remember?"

I unclench my fists and pick up my pen.

"Sorry," Candace says, and she puts her head down on the table. I don't even feel bad for her because who goes around asking about people's moms and how they died? And I'm mad that I don't have an answer. I don't know exactly how my mom died, so even if I wanted to talk about it, I couldn't.

"Why don't you write down your mom's name on your list?" Derek taps his finger on my list of important family members, right beneath Grandpa. "Because no matter what, she was important. If it weren't for her, you wouldn't be here."

And I'm thinking that if *I* weren't here, my mom probably would be.

But I do what Derek says, and just writing it out makes me feel a little better.

Important People in My Family:
Grandpa
Edna Rose Miller

Then I start to draw one of those family trees you see in textbooks sometimes, or on the first page of really complicated books with too many characters. I start with Grandpa and make the tree from there until I have everyone Grandpa told me about and I'm starting to feel like maybe I could do this project.

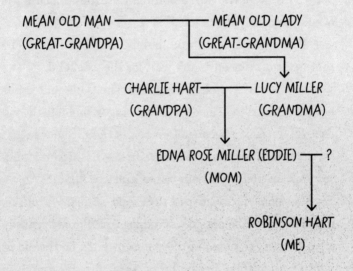

MEAN OLD MAN ————————— MEAN OLD LADY
(GREAT-GRANDPA)   (GREAT-GRANDMA)

CHARLIE HART————— LUCY MILLER
(GRANDPA)   (GRANDMA)

EDNA ROSE MILLER (EDDIE) —— ?
(MOM)

ROBINSON HART
(ME)

I don't really want to include my grandma Lucy's mean parents, the ones who thought Grandpa wasn't good enough for their daughter, but I do anyway because it makes it look like I have more family, so if Ms. Meg bends over my work she doesn't have any reason to linger around and try to help me.

Derek leans over and says, "Look at all those people!" and he puts his hand up for another high five when Ms. Gloria pokes her head in.

"Robbie, Candace, Oscar?" she says. "Bring your

projects." She winks at me because this was my idea, that we work on our family trees together.

I nod to Derek and close my notebook. "Oh," I whisper. "This weekend we're boiling. Saturday morning is Maple Day. Tell your mom."

"Yes!" Derek says and pumps his fist. "We'll be there!" And I already can't wait for the weekend.

Candace lifts up her head from the table and grabs her book bag. I guess now I'm starting to feel a little bad that she feels bad because Derek was right. She was just trying to be nice. So when we're in the hall I run a step to catch up and walk next to her and say, "It's OK."

She looks up from the floor and smiles. "Thanks, Robbie." Then she pats my shoulder, and I'm not usually a touching-type person unless it's Grandpa or Harold or Paul or sometimes Derek, but it feels OK, so I don't say anything.

We start with a check-in, but Ms. Gloria says we'll get to use the rest of our time to work on our projects.

Alex's chair is empty, and I can't believe his mom actually let him stay home from school today, especially since we have tomorrow off anyway. I guess she's way cooler than she seems, because I don't know anyone else's mom who would do that.

"I'm a three," Candace says, which is her all-time

low. "Stuff's just hard right now."

Then she passes the talking wand to me. I turn it back and forth in my hands, but then I decide to do what Candace always does because I think she might want to say more but just needs a little help to do it. "Are you sure you don't want to say anything else?" I reach the wand back out to her in case she wants to take it again.

And maybe it's because I asked her nice, or maybe it's because Alex is absent, so there's no one to laugh and break all the group norms and make everyone feel crappy, but Candace reaches back for the talking wand and says, "OK."

She pulls a little on the bottom of her shirt and shifts in her chair. It's kind of hard to see her face from underneath the brim of my hat, and I actually do want to hear what she says, so I turn it around backward. Ms. Gloria nods at me and smiles, and that feels pretty OK too.

Then Candace taps the wand on her knee and says, "My sister and I used to be really close. Best-friends kind of close."

She takes a deep breath and I can tell she's trying not to cry, and I hope she doesn't because I suck at being around crying people. It makes me feel awkward and like I'll do something wrong. Like holding a baby. But I guess I did OK at that with May. So I take a deep breath too and just keep listening.

"She started high school this year and got all these new friends who don't want to hang out with me because I'm just some fifth grader. They'd rather wear makeup and message their friends on their phones and make fun of me for being chubby."

Then she does it. She starts crying, and it's not awkward at all, just like it wasn't awkward to hold May. It's OK, and I actually kind of feel like I could cry right with her about Grandpa and my mom and how Grandpa packed up his bags and he didn't even know why. But I blink my eyes really fast and look away from Candace and think about baseball, and then I don't have to cry anymore.

"She's just so mean now. And she and my mom are always screaming at each other. I miss the old her." Then she passes the wand back to me and says, "Thanks, Robbie."

"That sounds like it really sucks," I say. "Sorry."

Ms. Gloria looks at me and smiles and I know what she means. She means *good job, Robbie* because even though I said *sucks* I helped Candace share and I followed all the norms.

"I'm a seven," I say. "I found out my mom's name, and it's Eddie." I want to say more about Grandpa and all the questions I have left to ask him before it's too late, before his memory wears out and all that information gets locked up tight in his brain. But I think I know what happens to an eleven-year-old when her only branch snaps, so I don't say anymore.

And all of a sudden I'm feeling more like a five or a six than a seven.

I pass the talking wand to Oscar.

Oscar's a six because he and his mom just finished unpacking boxes from their move. "Finally," he says. He's still talking to the ground, but he's loud enough to hear, and Alex isn't there to say something mean. He tells us he misses his dad a lot, but every time they hang out it kind of stinks because his dad talks crap about his mom. "And my mom says all this bad stuff about my dad too. Like I'm supposed to pick a team or something," he says.

He hands the wand back to Ms. Gloria, and she says that she's a seven today because she's sad to hear about some of the hard things going on in our lives but so happy that we are talking through them together.

She also tells us she's looking forward to tomorrow, when all the teachers have a big planning day and the students don't come to school. "We'll be preparing for our big family open house next week."

Oscar laughs a little under his breath and says, "We're looking forward to it too. No school!"

Ms. Gloria smiles. "I bet." She says she's looking

forward to meeting all our families next week. And I'm thinking she's already met Grandpa. Too many times. But I'm not telling Grandpa about any family open house after school anyway.

"Robinson had a great idea yesterday that we could work on our family trees together here in Group Guidance," Ms. Gloria announces.

"Yes!" Candace says.

Oscar nods his head.

"OK, then," Ms. Gloria says. "I'll let you guys work. Let me know if you need anything." She goes to her desk in the corner of the room and takes out her own notebook and a pen.

Candace lays out her poster board on the table in front of us. "How do you think I should arrange these?" she asks as she spreads out a whole bunch of pictures of her family members.

"Which one is your sister?" I ask.

She picks out three pictures. "This one is us at our aunt's house after our first day of swim lessons," she tells me, pointing at the first one. "This is us in our matching Christmas pajamas three years ago. And this one is the most recent. It's the first day of school. Fifth grade for me, ninth for her. My mom always makes us take first-day pictures."

In each picture they have their arms around each

other and are smiling big.

Then she slides over another picture. "This is her ninth-grade class picture."

It makes me feel bad to see the last picture because I can see how much she's changed, which I know makes Candace sad. In the last picture her hair is dyed white blond with two purple streaks down the sides, and she's wearing black makeup around her eyes and bright pink on her lips.

"My mom says she's just adjusting to high school. But they yell at each other all the time. My dad rolls his eyes and says, 'Teenagers,' and my mom rolls her eyes at him and tells him he should be doing more as a father. I hate it all so much."

"What's her name?"

"Tessa."

"Maybe you should put the pictures of Tessa and you at the middle of your project," I suggest.

Then Oscar adds in, "And her ninth-grade class picture could be at the top. You know, like you're all supporting her or something. Like holding her up. Even if she's kind of being different and mean. Like you'll be there for her and love her anyway."

That's definitely the most I've ever heard Oscar talk. And though I'm not going to say it out loud, I like his idea even better than mine.

"I like that," Candace says. "Maybe I could make all my family members into, like, some kind of net at the bottom or something, like we'll be there when she decides to stop being so mean. You know, like those safety nets at the circus or something."

Oscar and I nod and Candace starts arranging the pictures of Tessa on her poster board. "Thanks, guys."

As I watch her sorting through her family I wish that Grandpa had pictures of Eddie. I always wondered why he didn't at least keep one. Even if he put it somewhere secret where he didn't have to see it every day and get sad by remembering.

Oscar's sketching two trees on a blank page in a cool-looking black leather notebook. In the middle of the two trees he starts drawing a picture of himself, and it's really good. Each time he swipes his pencil across the page, the drawing looks more and more like him. He sketches himself with his arms stretched out between the two trees.

Then he catches me staring. "One tree is my mom's side and the other is my dad's," he explains.

I'm thinking this kid is some kind of genius. "Is everything you do always this deep?" I ask.

He laughs, and I guess that means yes.

All this time Ms. Gloria's working on her own family tree project. She's cutting something out of blue construction paper.

"You have to do this project too?" I ask her.

She laughs. "I guess I don't have to." She presses a glue stick into the construction paper. "But it's good to reflect on family every once in a while."

Everyone has some kind of creative idea, even Ms. Gloria, and I don't. All I have are boring lines and the names of some people I don't even know.

For the rest of the period I help Candace smear the glue stick across her poster board and press down the pictures of her and her sister.

When the bell rings we all start to pack up our projects and Ms. Gloria says to have a great long weekend and she'll see us Monday. And I'm thinking how I'll get to spend all day tomorrow in the garage helping Grandpa, then on Saturday we'll boil sap, which is about the most perfect weekend I can think of.

"Hey, Robinson," Ms. Gloria says, and I turn around before I push open the door. "So it went OK with your grandpa?"

I nod. "But I've got more questions."

She smiles and gives me a thumbs-up. That's when I see the beginning of her project, blue birds cut out of construction paper, flying in a V across her white poster board. But there's one bird that's not in the V, one who's flying off in a different direction alone.

I didn't know that a teacher's family could be not perfect. I never really thought about the fact that Ms. Gloria had a family. And I wonder if that was Ms. Gloria flying off by herself and where she was going.

chapter 17

The fire is burning hot in our backyard pit on Saturday morning by the time I hear Derek and his mom pull into our driveway in their Subaru Outback. I peer around the house and see Derek open the passenger door and jump out before his mom even puts the car in park.

"Maple Day!" he screams and runs out to the yard with his purple mitten up the whole way, ready for a high five.

His mom follows behind him, walking carefully through the snow in her big boots. She looks just like the adult version of Derek—short, twig skinny, all bony elbows and knees, and off balance.

"Welcome!" Grandpa calls and walks over to help Derek's mom through the melting snow.

Yesterday in the garage Grandpa and I did two car inspections, three oil changes, and put new tires on a Toyota Prius. All without Harold. And Grandpa talked with customers and didn't get his words crossed either.

"Glad you could make it," he tells Derek's mom.

"Are you kidding? There's no way we'd miss an invitation to boil sap," she says. "Derek talks about this all year."

Today is going to be another good day just like yesterday.

The flames from the fire pit are burning high up over the brick walls that are sunk into the ground. I know that high flames mean it's time for another couple pieces of dry, split wood from our pile.

"Come on." I pull Derek toward the shed. "Let's get your gloves." Derek and his mom have boiled with us for so many years that we keep a pair of gloves for both of them in the shed.

Derek's mom pulls on her work gloves and sits down on the stump chopping block. She helps sometimes, but mostly she likes to watch and take pictures of Derek and me.

"More wood," I order, and Derek and I race to the woodpile. I hold my arms out palms up while he stacks two pieces on my forearms to carry back to the fire.

Derek's always too scared to throw another piece of

wood on the fire, so that's my job every time. Grandpa pokes at the burning wood in the pit and says, "OK, Robbie." That's my cue that I can throw the next piece on and step back fast because the sparks fly up and you don't want them to catch your clothes.

Grandpa's bringing over the metal bars that stretch across the fire and the big lobster pot we'll use to boil. His brain is hardwired for boiling, so he's remembering all the steps, and his memory doesn't seem tired at all, which is good because there's no reason for Derek's mom to raise her eyebrows.

Grandpa puts the lobster pot on the metal bars and the fire starts to heat up the bottom. Then he lets Derek pour the sap from our gallon jugs into the pot until it's three-quarters of the way full.

"Now we wait," Derek says.

Grandpa nods. "Until the staff boils down to half."

And I know he means *sap*. I look quick at Derek and his mom to see if they noticed, and I don't think they did, but I can't tell.

"Then I get to add more sap. Right, Mr. Hart?" Derek asks.

Grandpa nods again and stirs the sap with the big slotted spoon we brought out from the kitchen.

Derek wants to make a snowman while the sap's boiling, but the whole time we're rolling the snow across the yard I'm watching Grandpa as he sits next to Derek's mom on the stump chopping block. I wonder what they're talking about or if they're talking at all and if Grandpa's words are staying straight, so I keep pushing the snow toward them to see if I can spy in.

"Beautiful day." I can hear Derek's mom's voice. "Perfect for boiling, isn't it?" she asks. "Derek always starts getting excited when it's cold at night and warms up during the day. Nothing he loves more than Maple Day." Grandpa nods.

"That's right," I cut in. "Grandpa taught me to recognize perfect sap-running weather when I was little." I stand up from the big snowball we're pushing around for the base of our snowman. "And I taught Derek."

Grandpa slides his work gloves off his hands, lays them on the ground by the stump, and says, "I bet we'll get a few more . . ." Then he looks like he looked the night he wandered off, except this time it's his sentence that wanders off and he can't follow it.

". . . A few more boiling days before the end of the season," I finish for him.

Derek's mom smiles. "Well, that's great! Your syrup is the best in all of Vermont, Charlie." And that's true. And that's saying something.

Derek points to the corner of the yard. "Let's set up our snowman over there."

We push our big snowball across the yard, collecting more and more snow as we roll, and it gets big fast, so by the time we get it over to the corner of the yard it's up past my knees. But it's also far from the stump chopping block, where Grandpa's forgetting the ends of his sentences, and I can't make a snowman and spy in on him at the same time.

Derek's asking me about how deep into the woods the hiker's shelter on the Appalachian Trail is from here and saying maybe he'll go with us one day this summer. I want to tell him it's only a mile, though he'd still never make it, but I'm trying to listen to Grandpa from across the yard.

Then I hear Derek's mom squeal. "Oooooo!"

When I look over, the pot is bubbling over and making hissing sounds. Grandpa stands up quick and Derek and I run over fast. I can tell by the look on Grandpa's face that he forgets this step, he forgets what to do if it boils over.

Even Derek's mom remembers. "Did you bring out the vegetable oil?" and she's running to the kitchen in her big boots, all slow and off balance while Grandpa is frozen to his spot.

"Lift it off," I tell him. "Lift off the pot, Grandpa."

And before I know it he's reaching for the big metal handles on the pot except his gloves are still in the snow next to the stump and I try to shout, "Wait!" in time but I don't because Grandpa's yells are filling the cold air and the pot is overturned and spilling sap into the snow.

Derek is screaming now too.

And Grandpa's shaking his hands and tears are streaming down his face and getting all caught up in his deep grooves.

"Oh my God, Mr. Hart! Mom! Mom!" Derek yells.

She hasn't even gotten to the front door yet and now she's running back and yelling. "What happened?"

I hold Grandpa's elbow and tell him to sit in the snow and he kneels down slow and then sits crisscross apple-sauce like we learned in pre-K. I make a snowball and tell him to hold it. And I keep saying I'm sorry, I'm so sorry, because if I hadn't told him to lift the pot, then his hands wouldn't be screaming red and he wouldn't have to cry in front of Derek and Derek's mom and if I had remembered the vegetable oil in the first place I would have added a few drops in the foam and it would have simmered down like Grandpa taught me when I was a little kid and if I hadn't been so far away making a stupid snowman in the corner of the yard, then none of this would have happened.

Derek's mom tries to look at Grandpa's hands, but he pulls them away.

"It's nothing," he mumbles. "Just a stupid mistake."

His brain is supposed to be hardwired for this. Hard-wired for boiling sap into maple syrup, hardwired for all the steps and details.

I hand him another snowball and he holds it between his hands. I can tell they're stinging bad, because he squeezes his eyes closed tight as the snowball melts.

"Charlie," Derek's mom insists, "let me see." And she reaches out again for his hands. She uncurls his fingers and looks at his palms.

"I'm really fine. It's nothing." He wipes his cheeks with the sleeve of his red flannel shirt.

"It looks like a first-degree burn," she says. "Let's go inside and treat this before it gets worse."

Derek is kind of crying and he's sniffling and wiping the snot off his nose with his work gloves. That's what happens when Derek gets scared. He starts crying and doesn't know what to do. That's why I play third base and he stands behind me.

"I saved some of the sap." He sniffles. The pot is right side up again in the snow, and the fire is still burning hot flames from the brick pit.

"Good job, Derek," I say because I don't want to ruin his day too. That makes him smile, which makes things feel a little more OK. But not really.

We're following his mom and Grandpa inside when I remember that we're not supposed to leave the fire blazing if we're not outside to watch it. I don't want to put it out because it'll take too long to start it all over again and that means that Maple Day is ruined for good. But I don't want to stay outside with it while Grandpa's inside with his stinging hands and Derek's mom's asking him questions. So I take a shovel of sand from the bucket in the shed and carry it out to the yard and dump it on the flames until they die out.

When I get inside Derek's mom is holding a cold cloth on Grandpa's hands. Then she rubs some lotion on his palms and tells him he might want to take some Advil for the swelling. Derek's dad is a doctor. I wonder if that's how she knows all this stuff. Or maybe it's just that she's a mom, and moms know stuff.

"Thank you," Grandpa says. "And Derek, don't you worry. Melted day will . . ."

And I know he means *maple*, and his face looks lost again.

"Maple Day will happen again soon. Maybe next weekend." I look at Derek and his mom. "We'll collect more sap to boil by then anyway."

"Wouldn't miss it!" Derek says. "I'm sorry about your hands, Mr. Hart."

I walk them to the door, and Derek's mom says she'll call to check on us tomorrow. "And please call me for anything." Then she's taking a long look at Grandpa. "Let me write my number down just in case," she says, and I know she's worried because she's raising her eyebrows and wrinkling up her forehead and her eyes look really sad. "Make sure he keeps those hands moisturized. Call if you see any blisters that are bigger than your pinkie fingernail."

Derek's mom pats my shoulder, and before I know it my eyes are getting all burny and I have to blink really fast and look up at the ceiling so I don't cry like some baby.

"You're taking good care of him, Robbie."

I shake my head like that's not true because it's not. "He takes care of me."

chapter 18

On Monday morning I'm trying to braid my own hair before school so I don't make Grandpa's hands worse, but no matter how many times I start over I can't keep all the pieces tied in tight and my curls end up popping out and spilling down to my shoulders. And there is no way I'm wearing my hair down like that to school. I try to pull it back in just a ponytail, but I hate the way the loose ends feel brushing on my neck and I don't want to wear it any different because then everyone will make a big deal about it and it's just stupid hair.

"Need some help?" Grandpa's poking his head in my bedroom.

"But your hands—"

"They're good as new." He opens and closes his

fingers to prove it.

But I know they're not good as new because I spied on them last night when he was sleeping. One hand was flung to the side over his bed and the other was across his chest. I used my hiking headlamp to examine each palm, turning them over softly in my hands so he didn't wake up, and making sure they didn't have any blisters bigger than my pinky fingernail like Derek's mom said. They were red and puffy and looked as hot as the flames from the fire pit.

"Here, turn around," Grandpa says, and he grabs the comb from my dresser and starts dividing my hair in two even parts.

"Maybe I'll just cut off all my hair," I tell him, imagining how good a buzz cut would feel. "I don't know if I'd look stupid, though."

Grandpa snorts a little laugh and bends over my shoulder and kisses my cheek. Normally I say *ewww* when he does stuff like that, but it feels pretty OK this morning, so I just stay quiet.

"I know for a fact," Grandpa says, "you'd look great."

"You can't know for a fact."

He's braiding the left side, pulling each section tight over and over, but I can tell his hands are fumbling more than usual, which means my curls might start popping out before the end of the day.

"Eddie always wore her hair short," he says. I can't believe Grandpa said her name like it was so easy all of a sudden.

"How short?" I ask.

"Boy short. Quarter inch off her head, if that."

And I'm picturing my mom walking down the street and everyone's moving out of her way because she's that tough. And she's giving people fist bumps and nodding with a quick jut of her chin to say *what's up?*

Grandpa asks for the rubber band. I hand it to him and he wraps it around the bottom of my first braid.

"Grandpa?" I try. "What happened to my mom? I mean, I know she—but what exactly—"

"Enough of that, Robbie," he cuts in. "Time for school." His voice is hard, but I don't give a crap because she's my mom and I should get to know how she died. I should get to see pictures and hear all about her. I don't have the guts to tell Grandpa that all of this is bull crap and he has to start telling me stuff before he can't remember anything anymore, so I just huff loud and sit there.

He hurries through my second braid and ties the rubber band. It's not tight like it's supposed to be. It's rushed and loose, and I can feel it unraveling hair by hair before I even grab my book bag.

• • •

At school Ms. Meg reminds us that our projects are due Thursday. "And what's even more exciting," she announces, "is that your teachers have planned a fun open house for your families and you'll be presenting your family tree projects as part of it!"

She starts passing out neon blue fliers. One lands in front of me on my table.

YOU'RE INVITED!
Please join us for an open house on Thursday, March 24, in Ms. Meg's classroom.
Student presentations begin at 3:30 p.m.

I crumple the blue piece of paper into a tight ball and flick it off my table. No way am I presenting my family tree project in front of anyone. Derek dives onto the floor and picks up the crumpled flier fast before Ms. Meg can get on my case.

"Put this in your book bags right now so you don't lose it," Ms. Meg shouts over everybody else's excitement. "And don't forget to tell your families!"

Not going to happen.

Out of the corner of my eye I see another crumpled blue paper fly. It came from Alex's table, and he's leaning back in his seat with his arms crossed over his chest. He's wearing a hat today too, which he never does, probably because he's so proud of his flowy, feathery hair, and the brim is pulled down low over his face like mine.

Usually an open house would be another chance for him to show off his perfect life and make fun of other people's projects under his breath. But he just sits there looking down at his shoes. And I remember how he shook and sobbed in Ms. Gloria's room. I guess even bullies might have crap going on.

Everyone else is working on their projects, and all of them are creative and good. Eric is making a tall 3-D tree out of popsicle sticks and Amy brought in an actual potted plant and is hanging little drawings and names off the leaves. The Chelsea/Brittany girls have papier-mâché trees taller than baseball bats planted in the back of the room, and now they're wearing matching pink smocks and covering the floor with newspaper to paint the trees green.

I don't have anything else but what I scribbled in my notebook last week. Just names of people I know nothing about. And I can feel my hair poking out from the right braid, which Grandpa rushed through, and I wish I could tighten it up or chop it off.

I don't even hear Ms. Gloria creak open the classroom door because everyone is so excited about their projects that they can't even talk like normal people. Everything is a squeal or a scream.

Ms. Gloria catches my eye and motions toward the door like she's asking if I want to get out of here. I grab my stuff. "See you later," I say to Derek.

"Meet you on third base," he says.

I follow Alex, Oscar, and Candace down the hall to Ms. Gloria's room, where at the very least it'll be quieter.

Ms. Gloria says we're going to do a quick check-in, then she'll give us time to work on our projects together again. Alex has the talking wand, and I'm waiting for him to tell us all about his day off from school last week and how great his four-day weekend was, and how he's so much cooler than we are. But instead he yells, "I'm an effing zero!"

My jaw actually drops because I'm pretty sure Ms. Gloria knows what *effing* means.

Then he passes the wand to Oscar, but Oscar just stays quiet for at least a whole minute because we're all still watching Alex.

The brim of Alex's hat is pulled down far over his face and his shoulders are shaking and he's making these loud huffing sounds. Candace stands up and stretches all the way across the table and pats his shoulder. She can barely reach him, and the edge of the table is digging into her belly, but she keeps patting his shoulder and says, "It's OK."

At first I'm kind of mad because Candace is supposed

to be our friend, and not nice to a bully like Alex, but then Alex pulls his knees up to his chest and cries loud with his whole body heaving hard. It's like watching that fancy BMW lose control again and drive wild into a brick wall, all its parts coming loose and fluid leaking all over the pavement.

"It's OK," Candace keeps repeating. "You can talk to us."

Alex sniffs and says between choking sobs, "You think I want to talk to you?" He shakes his head and mumbles. "I don't want to talk to some dumb, fat girl."

Candace pulls her hand from his shoulder and I'm trying to count to ten, but I don't make it past three because Candace already has her sister and her sister's friends calling her chubby and she's just being nice to Alex, which she doesn't even have to do.

"You jerk!" I shout. "You're crying like a baby and you still can't even be nice? What the *eff* is wrong with you?" I figure if he can say *eff* I can say it too.

Ms. Gloria stands and claps her hands one time really loud and we all look up. Her windshield-washer-blue eyes are no-nonsense, and I'm sure I'm about to get it because I'm always the one who gets in trouble. But instead she says to Alex, "We can see that you're hurting, Alex, and we are all sorry for that and want to help, but that doesn't mean that you can lash out at others. That's not right."

"Whatever," he sniffs.

"Not whatever," she demands. "Turn your hat around." Alex does it slowly and his face is a mess, red, with tears and snot running everywhere.

"You're not obligated to tell us what sadness you have in your life right now," Ms. Gloria tells him. "That's your business to share if you want. But you do owe Candace an apology for being mean to her."

"Sorry," Alex mumbles under his breath.

"A real one," Ms. Gloria says. "When it's real and you actually feel sorry, that's when you should apologize. We are here to listen whenever you are ready."

Ms. Gloria nods to Oscar, who is still holding the talking wand and I'm wondering if we're just going to go on like Alex isn't sniffling and blubbering. How can a kid whose mom gives him a new snowboarding jacket every year, and a whole day off school for no reason, be crying so hard?

Oscar starts to say that he's a seven because now he at least has an idea for his project and it doesn't feel so bad to work on it, when Alex interrupts. He's not even holding the talking wand, but no one says anything because he's crying so hard we can hardly understand him.

"I'm sorry!" he yells. "I'm really sorry! I mean it!"

Oscar hands Alex the talking wand, and all that power locked up inside with the purple and silver glitter falling from top to bottom must have made him feel safe to share, because he starts blubbering everything.

"My dad—cancer—moved his bed—living room downstairs—" He's gasping and sputtering between every few words and grabbing his stomach and doubling over and crying so much it sounds like he can hardly breathe and his back is shaking like crazy.

Candace gets up and walks around the table to stand next to Alex's chair. She's rubbing her hand across his back now and I'm not even mad at her for being nice to a bully because I want anyone to do anything that will make him stop crying like that.

He's still sobbing hard, and his words come choking out. "Thursday I had to stay home from school—alone with him—Mom had school conference for my brothers and—can't be alone." He lays his head on the table and just keeps crying big, big cries.

And then I do something I never thought was possible. I feel bad for him. I feel so bad for Alex Carter. I imagine him sitting with his sick dad all alone. *Cancer* is a scary word that I never had to think about for too long before, but Alex is sobbing so hard and no one can get him to stop. He probably thinks about it every minute.

"They say three months." Alex trembles.

That's probably why there were so many pills in his mom's car. They were for his dad.

"Thank you for sharing with us," Ms. Gloria says. "That was brave." Then she reaches over and touches his shoulder, and Candace is still rubbing his back. Oscar reaches over too and touches his other shoulder. And before I know it, I'm reaching out over the table and pressing my hand firm but nice on Alex's shoulder too. And we all just stay there quiet like that until Alex's shoulders aren't bouncing so hard up and down from crying anymore.

chapter 19

The whole walk to the garage after school I'm thinking about Alex and wondering if he's going home to sit with his dad and what they talk about and why some people get cancer and others don't and why some people can't remember and others can.

"Robbie!" Harold's walking out of the garage and wiping his hands on a towel, waving at me. "How was school? You staying away from trouble?"

I nod yes, and it's true. I haven't gotten in trouble since I slammed Alex to the lunchroom floor. And even thinking about that now makes me feel kind of bad after seeing him cry so hard and thinking about his dad who has to have a bed downstairs in the living room because he's too weak to walk upstairs anymore.

Harold gives me a fist bump and puts his arm around my shoulder. "How's May?" I ask. "I didn't think you'd be back for a while."

"She's great," he says. "Sleeping and pooping like a champ, so I figured I could come in and help out here while Paul holds down the poop fort at home today."

"Ew, Harold."

Harold was supposed to take a whole month off to take care of May, and it hasn't even been a week since she was born. It makes me nervous that he's here. I'm Grandpa's right hand, so he should know that I've got everything under control.

"There's a Jeep Grand Cherokee whose engine won't turn over. I could use some help," he says.

I nod OK.

The Jeep is parked in the first bay, and Grandpa is vacuuming out the backseat of a Toyota Avalon in the bay next to that.

"There she is," Grandpa says when he sees me, and turns off the vacuum.

"Hi, Grandpa."

"How was school?"

I want to tell him that it would be better if I knew more about my mom and could finish this family tree project already, but I just say, "Fine."

"She's going to help me with this Jeep," Harold tells him.

Grandpa smiles and nods and starts the vacuum again.

It doesn't take a rocket scientist to figure out that the Jeep Grand Cherokee's connecting cables are corroded. I hold out my hand to Harold and say, "Scalpel." That's another one of our things, like the fist bumps. He puts a wire brush in my palm and helps me disconnect the cables from the battery. I have to lean in far to reach the battery, but I remember when I used to have to kneel on the bumper to reach. I'm big enough now that I don't have to do that anymore. While I'm cleaning the end of the cable with the brush, Harold leans in with me and whispers. I can hardly hear him over Grandpa's vacuum.

"Hey, how's your grandpa been feeling?"

"Fine," I say, and keep on scrubbing with the wire brush so when we connect it back to the battery the engine will turn over good as new.

"How'd that happen to his hands?"

"It was an accident."

Harold takes hold of the cables and helps me connect them back to the battery. Then he starts to loosen the other side from the starter just to make sure they aren't corroded there too.

I lean in farther and he leans in with me and right there under the hood he says, "Robbie, I know he's having a hard time." He pats my work glove with his work glove, and I grip the wire brush tight. I don't know if it's because it feels kind of safe under the hood of a 2011 Jeep Grand Cherokee or the hum of Grandpa's vacuum makes him feel farther away, or if it's because Harold's voice is calm and real like Ms. Gloria's is, but before I know it I'm telling him everything.

I'm telling him about Grandpa's flannel shirt folded up with the pots, and about him wandering past our sugar maples. I'm telling him about his suitcase packed up like he might follow an old idea drifting around his head right out the door at any minute, and about the aloe plant I carried home from Dean and Walt's country store to squeeze and rub into his palms at night.

Harold pats my work glove with his again and I'm trying to connect the cables back to the starter, but there are tears blurring up my eyes and I can't. "Here," he says, and takes the cables. "I got it. Let me help." He connects them.

I want to tell him that I don't need help. That I can connect cables back to a starter easy and that Grandpa and I are just fine on our own.

Even though the cables are connected and it's time to try the engine, Harold doesn't close the hood of the Jeep.

We stay there bent over the engine and battery, the oil, and all the tubes and sparks that make everything work right, and Harold tells me that Derek's mom called him and sounded worried after our failed boiling day.

At first I'm mad that she went sticking her nose in our business, but after telling everything to Harold I feel a little lighter somehow.

Grandpa turns off the vacuum and calls, "How's that engine running now?" We stand up fast and Harold slams down the hood of the car.

"About to check it, Charlie," he says and hands me the keys.

When I try the key, the engine turns over quick and easy. Good as new. And I wish there were some wire brush to clean out Grandpa's corroded cables and reconnect them to his starter so he could ride out good as new too.

"A-plus, Robbie," Grandpa says and pats my shoulder with his bandaged hand.

Before we leave, Harold slips a piece of paper into the fold of my baseball glove. "If you need anything, Robbie," he says. "Anything." His hair is wild and sticking up, and I think I can even see a few gray ones poking out in the front. "I'm here. Looking out for you."

His brown eyes are glassy and tired, and I wonder if May ever lets him sleep and I know already I won't call him. Harold's got his family to take care of. And I have mine.

On the walk home I'm wishing my hair wasn't so loose and touching my neck, and thinking that no more adults than Harold can find out about Grandpa's memory.

I take the keys from Grandpa's hand and slide the house key in the front door.

"Hang your flannel here, Grandpa," I tell him when we get inside and point to the black hook by the door.

"I know that," he gruffs. He unbuttons his flannel slowly, then takes off his boots.

"Tuna melts?" he asks. I nod yes and even though I'm pretending to get out my homework, I'm really watching him. Watching him walk to the kitchen and plug in the toaster oven, take out two English muffins and mayonnaise. Watching him get a fork from the drawer and a bowl to mix the tuna in.

Then I'm watching him look at the can of tuna fish. He picks at the can's edge with his thumbnail. Then he tries to pry it off with the fork. Then he slams it hard against the counter. "Dammit!" he yells.

"Grandpa!" I rush to take the can from him.

"Goddammit!" he yells again. "I don't need any help."

My heart's beating fast because it's scary when Grandpa's mad and he does need help but I don't want to make him feel like crap by showing him how to open the tuna. He was the one who taught *me* how to crank the can opener around a can of tuna fish when I was little. It would feel weird and wrong to teach him how to use it now.

I open the drawer and take out the can opener. "It's OK, Grandpa," I say and hold out my other hand. "I'll do it. I remember how you taught me. Just watch and make sure I do all the steps right."

He nods, but I can tell he's still mad because he's huffing big breaths through his nose. I click the opener onto the edge and twist it around the can until the top peels off.

"Good," he says. Then I empty the tuna fish into the bowl with a spoonful of mayonnaise.

Grandpa stirs it up while I toast the English muffins.

Before bed Grandpa unwraps the bandages from his hands and I snap another piece from the aloe plant and squeeze it on his palms.

And later that night when he's sleeping I sneak in again to make sure he hasn't packed up his suitcase to wander off, and to check on his hands. I pull back his wool blanket and as quiet and soft as I can I roll his big hand to face me. I rest my pinky finger soft in his big palm and there aren't any blisters bigger than my nail.

He smells like wood and wool and aloe and his hands look better than they did yesterday. I pull the blanket back up and tiptoe back to my bed, then listen to his deep breaths as I fall asleep.

chapter 20

The next day in Ms. Meg's class Derek takes out his board game family tree. It looks really good already, and it's not even due for two more days. His mom helped him paint a square piece of cardboard purple, and all the spaces around the edge where the game pieces go they painted in white. He's bent over our table writing on the game cards.

"When you land on a square that says *Take Card*, you pick a card and read about a family member. Then you get to add one of these plastic people to your side." He hands me a tiny plastic figurine. "The person who has the most family members by the end wins."

I guess I'm a huge loser, then.

"That's so cool!" Candace gushes.

Candace's project is full of pictures and is almost done too. She has two brown markers out to color the trunk of her tree.

I look down at the drawing I have in my notebook.

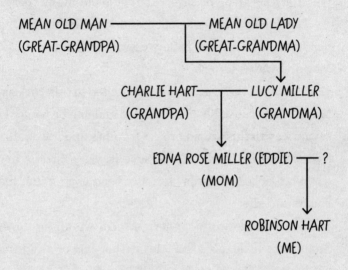

MEAN OLD MAN ——————— MEAN OLD LADY
(GREAT-GRANDPA)   (GREAT-GRANDMA)

CHARLIE HART——— LUCY MILLER
(GRANDPA)   (GRANDMA)

EDNA ROSE MILLER (EDDIE) —— ?
(MOM)

ROBINSON HART
(ME)

I grab one of Candace's brown markers, clutch it tight in my fist, and press a fat X over my whole stupid family tree. I roll the marker back to Candace, and she and Derek are staring at me with huge eyes.

"What?" I say.

"Do you want me to help you start over?" Derek asks.

I lean back in my chair and bury my hands in the pocket of my sweatshirt. "That's impossible," I say. "I don't even know these people. I don't have anyone to put on a family tree. Besides Grandpa."

Derek moves his foot over next to mine under the table and nudges my Nike Air Griffeys with the toe of his Converse.

"You know me," he says. "You could put me on there."

Then the door creaks open and Ms. Gloria's poking her head in. "I'm here for my crew." She smiles at Ms. Meg and waves us out.

The weird thing is, I'm almost excited to talk to Alex. Maybe it's because his life sucks too and maybe we could say no way to this stupid project together and it wouldn't feel so bad. Or maybe it's because it was a little scary when he sobbed yesterday and I've been hoping that his dad doesn't die.

When we get to Ms. Gloria's room we all sit down around the little table and Alex isn't crying or anything but he looks like he could at any second.

"How's your dad?" I ask.

"The same," he answers. "He's not going to get better, so the same isn't the worst, I guess."

I don't know what to say so I just say, "Sorry," and I do that thing that Derek does when I feel like crap. I slide my Nike Air Griffey toward his foot under the table and just leave it there, the sides of our shoes barely touching. Alex doesn't kick me in the shin or anything, so I figure it makes him feel pretty OK too.

"There's this counselor that comes to our house to talk to my mom and my brothers and me. He's OK," Alex says. "He told us it might be a good idea to write down the things we want to say to my dad and questions we want to ask him before—" His voice catches and his eyes fill up. "Before it's too late, I guess." He looks down.

"That sounds really hard," Candace says.

Oscar leans forward and says in his whisper kind of voice, "Sorry."

I realize that the talking wand is just lying in the middle of the table, and I think it really might be full of magic like Ms. Gloria said it was, because we're all just talking now and everything is going fine. Alex isn't being mean and no one is yelling or flicking bits of paper in anyone else's hair.

And I usually don't believe in magic, but if it does exist I wouldn't be surprised if Ms. Gloria caught some and sprinkled it in with the purple glitter in the wand because instead of wanting to shove or slug Alex Carter I can actually kind of understand how he feels, even if just a little bit, because I want to ask my Grandpa some things before he forgets the answers. But it's too late already. Every time I get to the topic he closes up tight.

"I'm proud of you all for opening up, and for your kindness to each other," Ms. Gloria says. "Kindness is the only thing that can make some of our hurt go away."

Then Alex turns to Candace. "Sorry I said you were fat before. You're not. I was just mad, I guess."

Then he's looking at me. "I won't call you Robin anymore."

I want to ask him, *and how about what you did to Derek?* but I just stay shut because I don't want to wreck his nice streak. It's quiet for a while, but it doesn't feel awkward. It feels pretty OK, actually.

Then Ms. Gloria ruins it. "Projects are due Thursday," she says. "That's two days! I can't wait for your presentations. So let's get to work."

Candace and Oscar take out their projects quickly and get right to work on the finishing touches. Alex and I just sit there with our arms crossed and our hats pulled around in front of our faces and at the exact same time say, "I'm not doing it."

It makes us giggle a little. Then we start cracking up and I try to stop, but I can't. Alex laughs so hard he falls out of his chair and even Oscar starts cracking up too, and he laughs ten times louder than he talks, which makes me laugh even harder, and before I know it we're all on the floor laughing so hard that we're crying too.

At first Ms. Gloria has her no-nonsense voice on, trying to get us off the floor and back to work, but even she breaks and starts laughing and her laughs are these low, deep hoots that rise up from her belly and take over her whole body. She laughs and laughs with us until tears stream from her windshield-washer-blue eyes down her cheeks. We laugh and laugh until we can't laugh anymore.

"Maybe laughter can help us through the hurt too," Ms. Gloria wheezes. "Kindness and laughter." She's wiping her eyes with the back of her hand.

We're all nodding our heads and clutching our middles. My stomach burns and even my cheeks hurt from smiling so wide.

"And I don't mean laughing *at* other people," Ms. Gloria says, and she directs it right to Alex. "But laughing *with* others."

Alex nods like he gets it, and I think he does. And I think I do too. Sometimes people feel so bad they want to make others feel worse. And sometimes people can be so angry at something inside that it spurts out everywhere, like a high-pressure radiator leak.

"Ms. Gloria, are you going to show us your family tree?" Candace asks.

She looks over toward her desk. "I can if you want," she says, and reaches over for it. "I'm not quite done yet either."

It's turning out pretty cool. She glued all the birds on the poster board into a flying V across the sky and wrote names on the wings in black Sharpie marker.

Gloria leads the flock. There's still that one smaller bird who's flying away from the V, off into the white of the poster board.

"Who's that?" Oscar asks and points to the little bird flying off.

Ms. Gloria runs her finger over the outline of the little bird. "That's my son, Devon."

Ms. Gloria explains to us how she was the oldest of her siblings and always felt like she was helping to take care of them and lead them on a good path. "That's why I made my family tree as a flying V. That's me out front," she says and points. "Leading the way." She shows each of her siblings, the birds following behind her, and her other two children.

"Devon passed away when he was eight." Her chin trembles when she tells us. "But I like to think of him flying high and making his own way."

"I believe he is too," Candace says. Ms. Gloria pats Candace on the back and smiles.

"In my next life, I'm coming back as a bird," Ms. Gloria tells us. "That way I can sing to all the people who were great and kind, and poop on all the ones who weren't."

And maybe it's because everything was feeling too sad and heavy or maybe it's because our teacher said *poop*. But before we know it we're all doubled over and bursting out laughing again.

"You better watch out!" Oscar blurts and points at Alex. "Someday when you're an old man hobbling down the street, Ms. Gloria might poop on you if you don't start being nice to everyone!"

And that gets us laughing even harder because Oscar is supposed to be the quiet one who whispers his responses and never says anything if he doesn't have to, and now we're picturing Ms. Gloria flying over Alex's head and white poop splattering on his perfect blond flowy hair.

Ms. Gloria lets out big wheezes to catch her breath and says, "OK, OK, you crazy crew. Ms. Meg will kill me if you don't have your projects ready for Thursday." She points to Candace's and Oscar's projects. "Let's get to work now."

Candace and Oscar start right in, but they're still giggling under their breath.

"I don't have anything," Alex says.

"Me neither."

I show him the Xed out family tree sketched in my notebook. "I don't even know these people, except for my grandpa."

Alex leans in to look, and I can tell he wants to ask me a million things. Like why my grandpa's black and I don't look it. And how my mom died and if I have a dad.

But he doesn't ask, which is good because I don't know most of the answers anyway and having these people on my project makes my whole family tree feel like a lie.

"I just don't want to think about family right now," Alex says, and pushes his notebook away from him across the table. Then his face gets sad and his voice gets shaky again. "But my dad always feels proud of me when I do my schoolwork."

I'm trying not to but I can't help picturing his dad and all the pills and the downstairs bed.

"We just have to do it, then," I tell him. And I push his notebook back across the table.

Alex looks up at me. "OK." Then he reaches out his hand and says, "It's a pact. We'll make our projects. Even if they stink."

"They're going to be so crappy," I laugh. And that makes him giggle a little again too.

I reach out and we shake hands, like it's the end of a long game that went into extra innings and we finally just called the game off because it got too dark.

"Thursday," I say.

"Thursday," he repeats.

Even though it's bad, I'll go home and copy my big lie family tree onto a piece of colored paper and be done with it. I didn't say it was going to be good. Just done.

Then the bell's ringing and it's time for recess and all

I want is third base and Derek backing me up.

Alex slaps me on the back. "Come on, I'll let you bat first."

And I'm feeling the best I can until I hear my name being called over the loudspeaker. "Robinson Hart, please report to the office. Robinson Hart to the office, please."

chapter 21

Ms. Gloria says she'll walk me to Principal Wheeler's. I bet because she knows if I go by myself I'd skip the office and run outside to recess anyway. And she's right. I would. Because Mr. Danny's probably unloading the bats and baseballs from the gym bags right now and I'm supposed to bat first.

We're walking side by side down the hallway and I'm thinking this is bull crap that I have to go to the office during recess and I didn't even do anything bad.

When I get close enough to look through the big glass window of the office I see Grandpa sitting there with Harold and I take off running. "What the—"

I burst through the door and I look right at Grandpa and yell, "I didn't do anything! I swear!"

Harold stands up fast and puts his arms around my shoulders and says, "I know you didn't, Robbie."

And now I'm wishing I didn't say one stupid thing to Harold under the hood of that 2011 Jeep Grand Cherokee because I'm afraid he told some other adult and now we could be in real trouble. He's supposed to be on my team.

There's a woman there I've never seen, wearing fancy black pants and a jacket and carrying a briefcase. I look at Ms. Gloria to give me an answer.

Then Principal Wheeler walks out of her office and says, "Hi, Robinson. Thank you for joining us." She's acting nice. Too nice. And it's making me more nervous because I don't want any meeting or anyone's help and I don't know who this fancy-black-pants woman is and why she has to be here.

"Why did you call my grandpa?" I ask Principal Wheeler. "Why is Harold here? I didn't do anything! They have to go back to work."

I shake out from under Harold's arms and put my hand on Grandpa's shoulder. "You can go," I tell him. "Nothing is wrong." And I'm thinking maybe if he leaves before anyone asks him a question, then we'll be OK and no one will think he can't take care of me anymore. Because he can.

Grandpa's telling me to calm down, but I can't, and I

don't even want to try.

"Hi, Robinson," the fancy lady says. "My name is Grace and I'm a counselor at the Department for Children and Families in Vermont." She reaches out to shake my hand.

"I don't care who you are!" I yell because the Department for Children and Families sounds serious and scary, and I want to get us out of here fast before she says anything else. "I have to walk my grandpa back to the garage now, where he belongs because he can fix everyone in this town's cars."

But that Grace lady just keeps on. "I'm here because I wanted to meet you and to talk—"

"No one asked you to come!" I shout.

I grab my grandpa's bandaged hand from his lap, but Harold squeezes my shoulder and says, "Actually, Robinson, I did. I asked Grace to come here."

It feels like a fastball in the gut because Harold really did quit my team and before I know it we're all shuffling into Principal Wheeler's private office. Grace, Ms. Gloria, Harold, Grandpa, and me.

We're sitting in a circle, but it doesn't feel like the circle in Group Guidance, and there's no talking wand. If there were, I'd take it first and tell everyone to *eff* off, and then I'd never pass it on because I don't want to hear what anyone else has to say. But grown-ups never let kids have the talking wand when they've made up their minds.

"Robbie," Harold says. "I called Grace because I care about you so much, and I care about your grandpa. He's my best friend." Harold's eyes are getting all leaky and his voice is catching. He brushes his hand through his sticking-up brown hair. "I want to help you and your grandpa make a plan."

"We don't need a plan!"

Then Grandpa sits up in his chair and clears his throat into his fist. "Robbie. My memory's not so good. And it's not getting better. You dessert—"

And I know he means *deserve* but everyone staring at him is making him nervous and stressed. I look up to see if Principal Wheeler or Ms. Gloria or that lady Grace noticed, and I'm pretty sure they did because their eyes look sad, and we don't need anyone feeling bad for us because we're fine.

"You dessert—" Grandpa tries again.

And I know he wants to say *I deserve more.*

"No, Grandpa," I interrupt. "That's not true. You're fine." It's not fair that everyone's making him feel lousy. This isn't his fault. I'm the one who made his memory so tired all these years, but I'm good at helping him now.

"I spent the morning with your grandpa," Grace says. "And he told me all about you."

"I don't give a crap what you talked about," I tell her. "My grandpa and I are fine. I know what people like you do. You take kids away from the only *effing* family they have!"

"Robinson!" Principal Wheeler's eyes are wide. "Watch your language, please. We are all here because we care about you and your grandpa Charlie."

I know that's the biggest load of bull crap yet because if they really cared they wouldn't want some counselor around whose job it is to take me away. They'd know that I'm the only one who can find him when he wanders and make him feel OK when he can't open a can of tuna fish. They'd know that I'm really good at finding his flannel and the ends of his sentences.

"I know you're feeling upset, Robinson. This isn't easy," Grace starts again. "But I'd like you to try to listen to what your grandpa and Harold are thinking. You might find that the plan sounds OK."

Before I know it I'm standing up and my hands are tightening into fists because I'm not listening to anyone's plan.

"Robinson," Grace says. "I'm not here to take you away from your grandpa."

I bite down hard on my back teeth. Ms. Gloria catches my eye and I'm counting down from ten and taking a deep breath for each number.

"Your grandpa told me you are a special kid," Grace says. "He told me how good you are at fixing cars and tapping maple trees. He says you are his biggest helper for a lot of things."

"I'm his right hand," I spout through clenched teeth. "Harold's his left."

Grace smiles when I say that. Then she keeps telling me that she's not here to take me away from my grandpa, but I know she is. That's their big plan. That's what people like her do. They want to take me away because they don't think he's a good grandpa and they don't think I can take good enough care of him. But I can. My heart's beating loud in my ears and I just want to get out.

"Maybe we should talk about this another time," Grace offers. "I could come visit you and your grandpa when you're feeling a little better."

"How about never?"

Then Grandpa says, "No need to be rude to this nice lady, Robbie."

Harold nods and pushes himself up from his chair. "Maybe another time is best," he adds. "I can be there anytime."

"I could come by the house tomorrow morning," Grace says. "I'll bring doughnuts and we can talk before you go to school?"

I'm about to say no way, not even the

crispiest-on-the-outside-softest-on-the-inside doughnuts could make me want to ever see this woman again, but Harold jumps in fast and says, "That sounds great. I'll be there."

Grandpa nods and pushes down hard on his thighs to get up from his chair.

"Can I go home with my grandpa now?" I ask Principal Wheeler. I'm thinking there's no way I can go back to class. Not even recess. I don't trust anyone around Grandpa without me there.

I can tell Principal Wheeler is about to say no and that I have to spend the rest of the day in school. So I stare at her hard and say, "I don't feel good. I can't go back to class." I fake a nasty cough and everyone kind of laughs and rolls their eyes and nods.

Ms. Gloria turns to Grandpa. "Mr. Hart, you should be very proud of Robinson's progress. She's been managing her anger and empathizing with others. I know this is tough on her, but I'm confident she'll do a great job listening tomorrow morning." She's looking right at me when she says that last part.

"Thank you," he says. "I know she'll lips . . ." He looks up toward the ceiling as if his words got caught up in his brain somewhere, but he squints his eyes, shakes his head, and gives up.

Ms. Gloria takes his hand in hers and smiles. "Thank

you for coming, Mr. Hart."

Then I hold his hand and he walks side to side, side to side, to the office door.

I know he meant to say *listen*. Not *lips*. *Listen*. He meant to say that I'll listen to him and listen to Harold and Grace, and I wonder what they did to make him so brainwashed. Grandpa can't really think that someone from the Department for Children and Families is going to help us. He just needs to go back to the garage with me. His wires are all crossed because he gets confused in the afternoon, but in the morning he'll be clear and good as new and there's no way he'll want some lady to take me away.

"Let's go to the garage, Grandpa," I say. "I'll help you with the cars."

But as we walk away from the school, my stomach feels all tied up in knots because I know I can't wait around for anyone else's plan.

On the way to the garage Harold keeps trying to explain why he called that lady and finally I blurt, "I don't want to talk about this right now!" which is something that Ms. Gloria taught me to say when I'm annoyed and don't want to listen, and I'm surprised how well it works because Harold just pats my shoulder and doesn't say another thing the whole walk.

I don't want him patting my shoulder, though. Not today. So I shrug away and start walking a little faster.

Grandpa's quiet too, and even though I don't want to talk about anything, the silence is making me feel antsy, so I'm glad when we get to the garage because I can pull on my gloves and get to work.

She Roll is parked outside the garage, and Paul is leaning on the truck with May in a backward-book-bag-looking thing on his chest. He's holding a white bag from Dean and Walt's. I can smell the hamburgers from here because they're that good.

"I thought there might be some hungry workers needing lunch," he calls, holding up the bag. And the fact that he's here makes me feel suspicious. Like he might be in on this plan too.

Grandpa reaches out and touches May's head softly with his big hands. "Still a tiny thing," he says.

"You'd be surprised how fierce she is. She's little but fierce." Paul smiles and May yawns and dribbles a big string of spit on his shoulder.

I go to touch May's head too, like Grandpa did, because I kind of feel like I have to because she didn't do anything wrong. But before I can get to her tiny curls she reaches out her little hand and grabs my finger way harder than I thought a baby could grab and she squeezes tight.

"I told you. She's fierce," Paul says.

May is clutching hard and it's making me laugh a little because I don't actually know how to get my finger out of her grip.

"Looks like you're stuck with her," Harold says.

Then Paul kisses her little fist and starts peeling her fingers off mine one by one. She cries a little when I get free but then pushes her face back into Paul's chest.

He hands the hamburger bag over to me. I take one and pass it to Grandpa and I'm still wondering if Paul is in on the Department for Children and Families bull crap plan too. So I don't ask him how she's rolling and point to the back of his falling-apart old Chevrolet like I always do.

I just eat my lunch in four big bites and say, "Thanks for the burger." Then I ask Grandpa what I can work on even though I kind of wish I could see if May would grasp her fist around my finger again because it felt pretty OK. But I'm mad at Harold and maybe even Paul too.

"Honda Civic needs new brake pads." Grandpa points to the first bay.

Harold pulls on his gloves too. "Robbie and I can tackle that together."

"I can do it by myself," I snap, even though I've only changed brake pads one other time. I know I can remember all the steps if I go slow.

And I don't want Harold's help.

Harold holds his hands up like *don't shoot*, gives Paul and May a kiss good-bye, and starts toward the next bay, where he has to take the winter tires off a Subaru Forester. "I'll be right here if you need—"

"I got it."

Paul starts putting May in her car seat and toots the horn on the way out. "Good to see you, Robbie! Let's hope she rolls all the way home!" he calls out the open window.

I give him a weak smile and start loosening the lug nuts on the front tires of the Civic. And because I'm not asking for help I get a jack. I have to hoist up the car and I can't do that without Harold helping me position the wheels over the lifts. But I'm good with a jack, so before I know it I've got the front wheels up off the ground all by myself and I'm squatting down and removing the lug nuts and pulling the wheels off nice and easy like they're supposed to go.

I spray the caliper bolts with WD-40 and I remember Grandpa telling me about checking the pressure on calipers. If the car is cool and at rest, they should move back and forth easy, but if they're under pressure they'll fly off when you remove the bolts. So I'm careful to stand to the side and check behind me before I fit the socket over the bolts.

I can't get them to move at first try, so I spray more WD-40 and give them another hard crank. I can feel the heat rise up in me, all the way from my belly through my clamped tight teeth and into my cheeks. I'm putting all my weight in and they won't budge and if I can't get these calipers off I can't replace the worn-out brake pads with new ones that stop on a dime. And before I know it I'm punching the stupid things. Punching them hard, and my knuckles are burning through my work gloves and my legs are cramping from squatting because I had to use a jack instead of the lifts but I don't care because bolts are supposed to loosen and they're stuck and stubborn and stupid and I can't get them free.

Then I feel a glove on my shoulder. Harold is squatting behind me like an umpire behind the catcher and trying to pull me away from the wheel.

"I almost got it!" I scream. "Leave me alone!"

"Robbie," he whispers. "Let's take a breath for a minute." He puts his arm around my waist and pulls me back. We both kind of topple on the smooth cement of the garage floor, but I fall mostly on him. My fist is throbbing, and there are tears on my cheeks that I don't even know how they got there.

I can tell Harold wants to laugh because he's biting his lip and smiling and because we're all sprawled out on the floor like a couple of idiots, but I'm not in the mood for laughing. Not with him. Not today. So I roll off him and stand up fast.

"Try this." He holds out a red-and-yellow can. "It's better than the WD-40. I swear by it."

I grab it and give it three hard shakes before squatting back down at the wheel and spraying it on the caliper bolts and giving them a good hard crank with the socket. My knuckles burn when I tighten my fist. The bolts still aren't moving. I'm biting down hard on my back teeth and holding my breath and I want to punch the stupid things again. Then Harold's glove reaches over my shoulder and pushes down on my sore knuckles.

"One. Two. Three," he counts and we give it a good strong turn together and finally, they come free.

We don't say anything after that, and I do the rest by myself, but I know Harold is watching from the next bay.

And the whole time I'm putting on the new brake pads and checking the brake fluid, I'm thinking about the Department for Children and Families and how I'm not waiting around for Grace to come with doughnuts and take me away from Grandpa.

No way.

chapter 22

I need my hair braided up tight before I go to bed, and I try to do it myself, but every time I do my hair falls all loose and out of the braid. It has to be tight for what I'm going to do.

I tap lightly on Grandpa's bedroom door with my hair down long over my shoulders "Grandpa?" I ask. "Will you braid my hair?"

I'm waiting for him to ask why I need it done now so late at night and not before school in the morning like I always do, but he just waves me in and tells me to stand in front of the mirror.

My heart's beating fast and I don't know if it's because at any moment I'm expecting Grandpa to see right through me, right into my whole plan, or if it's because he doesn't even notice anything out of the ordinary.

He combs my hair with his fingers and parts it down the middle, then gathers the right side, separating it into three pieces.

"Tight, Grandpa."

He smiles at me in the mirror and crosses the groups of hair over each other and pulls them tight to my scalp. Tears burn behind my eyes, but it also feels good to have it pulled tight and intertwined like nothing could get between the strands to loosen it up and make it fall apart.

I hand him a rubber band and he wraps it around the bottom of the first braid. Then he braids the left side, crossing the hair over and over and pulling it tight to my scalp.

"Thanks," I say. And before I close his bedroom door I stick my head back in and say, "Hey, Grandpa. Everything's going to be OK."

I want to say what I always say, that I'll see him in the morning, first thing. But I don't want to lie to Grandpa.

I'm waiting for him to remind me about Grace and Harold coming over with doughnuts before school, but

he just nods and smiles. "Sleep well, Robbie." And I wonder if he remembers.

"You too, Grandpa."

Wearing my outdoor clothes in bed feels weird. My jeans
keep twisting around all wrong and I can't get com-
fortable. It's dark and the wind is whooshing past my
window. I'm going over the plan in my head and looking
at my hiking pack leaned against the far wall. It already
has my sleeping bag in it so it kind of stands up on its
own. I repeat the plan again and again, step by step, in
my head to keep me awake until I hear Grandpa's snores
through the wall.

When the alarm on my watch beeps four thirty a.m.
I blink my eyes fast and let them adjust to the dark.
That was part of the plan so I don't fumble around and
wake up Grandpa. Then I push off my blanket, hoist the
pack over my right shoulder, and tiptoe through the hall
and downstairs. I lean my pack against the front door
and tiptoe to the kitchen.

The cupboards squeak even when I open them slowly
to feel for the loaf of bread. A slant of light shoots across
the floor from the refrigerator as I reach in for the cheese
slices. I make a sandwich and wrap it tight in plastic
wrap like Grandpa taught me so the cheese doesn't slide

around and off the bread. Then I turn on the water just enough that it's barely leaking out of the faucet to fill my water bottle as quietly as I can.

I grab the first-aid kit from the hall closet because Grandpa says you never go into the woods without it and stuff it in the pack on top of my sleeping bag. When I hoist the pack up this time, it feels way heavier than I thought it would. But I can carry it.

I adjust my headlamp around my head and pull on my boots, and just when I'm about to turn the doorknob I hear Grandpa cough and shift on his old mattress upstairs. Then I imagine him waking up and not knowing where he is or where I am and maybe packing his suitcase again and wandering off. And I won't be here to follow him and find him and bring him back home.

But I can't be here when Grace shows up to tell me her plan and take me away. And she'll be here soon. If I just disappear for the morning, disappear from Grace and the Department for Children and Families, I can come back and get Grandpa and then we can make our own plan.

Grandpa needs me with him. I'm his right hand.

The light on my watch glows 4:58. Two hours until Grace will be pounding on our door with doughnuts. I have to go.

I turn the knob quietly, but I just can't push the door

open and run. I try again to get the guts, but I can't. I can't leave Grandpa here with no one listening for his breathing and snores through the wall.

I need a new plan.

When I inch the pack off my shoulders, it hits the floor with a thud. "Crap!" I whisper and slap my hand over my mouth as I tiptoe back to the kitchen.

This time I make a sandwich with an extra slice of cheese and slather it with mayonnaise and mustard the way Grandpa likes. The other water bottles are out in the shed, so I fill Grandpa's soup thermos with water, even though it's heavy and will probably kill my shoulders in the pack. But we'll need it. And I can carry it. I grab the blanket off the back of the couch and stuff that in too.

Tiptoeing back up the stairs makes me nervous. I don't want to startle Grandpa because it's still dark and early and his wires will be all crossed and confused.

I knock softly on his bedroom door but he keeps on snoring. I knock a little louder and walk in. He snorts and rolls over. "What? What? Who is it?"

"It's me, Grandpa. It's Robbie."

"What?" He sits up on the edge of his bed and shakes his head, but he doesn't shake anything into place because he's calling me Eddie and wondering if I'm going to come to Vermont. "Eddie, Eddie," he pleads.

"Come stay with me in Vermont until the baby's born."

"Grandpa, it's Robinson." I take his hand and help him stand up. I want to remind him that my mom died so he'll snap out of it and stop calling me Eddie and go back to being normal. But I don't want to make him sad, so I just forget about it. "It's time to go," I say. "Come with me."

I pass him his clothes and he slouches into his shirt and pulls his pants up over his hips. "I'll teach you how to sugar," he says, "if you come."

"I know how to sugar, Grandpa. You taught me. Remember?"

He rubs the grooves on his forehead and pats me on the shoulder. "Eddie. I'm so glad you came. I can't wait to be a grandpa."

Then I realize he's talking about me. And for as many times as I've asked him to tell me what happened to my mom, it feels weird and wrong and a little scary having him talk about her now, when his memory is so tired.

He holds me tight and whispers in my ear, "I wanted to be there when you were growing up, Eddie." Then he squeezes me tighter in the hug and says, "But you're here now and I'm going to be the best damn grandpa in the world." Then he rubs my belly over my sweatshirt and jacket.

"You are," I tell him. "You are the best grandpa in the world." He nods his head and loosens his hug.

"Ready?" I ask and grab a pair of thick socks from his drawer. I put his hand on my shoulder to lead him downstairs to the front door.

"Ready," he says. His voice is gruff and sounds stale, like he hasn't cleared the morning out of it yet.

That's how his memory is too. It's clear by the time the sun comes up for breakfast and he's braiding my hair before school, but it clouds up again when it gets dark and it's time to make dinner and go to bed.

But we can't wait for the sun to rise and his memory to clear. We have to get out of here now. Then we'll be OK and Grandpa can help me think about what we'll do next.

"You're going to need your flannel and a jacket too, Grandpa."

I take his flannel from the hook, but when I turn back around he has one bare foot in his boot and he's trying to pull his sock over the muddy toe.

"Socks first, Grandpa," I remind him. "Socks, then boots." It makes me mad and sad again at the same time that he doesn't know that. How can he forget the simplest things? All the things he taught me when I was a little kid. He's just staring back at me like he doesn't understand, so I reach over and start unlacing his boot. "Socks first."

"Stop it," he huffs. "Stop it, dammit. I can do it."

His eyes are those deer-caught-in-the-headlights eyes, and I just want him to snap out of it and go back to being the grandpa who makes sense, because he scares me when he's like this. But we have to get out of here before Grace from the Department for Children and Families comes to take me away.

chapter 23

The snow crunches beneath our boots and our breath hangs heavy in the air.

"We're going for our little hike, Grandpa," I say. "You remember our favorite route? Up to the hiker shelter on the Appalachian Trail?"

The pack is digging into my shoulders already, and we haven't even made it out of the yard and into the woods.

"You came on the train?" he asks. He's crunching along behind me, side to side, side to side. "Let me take your bag, Eddie. You've come a long way."

"It's OK, Grandpa," I say. "I can carry it." I keep trudging a couple of steps ahead of him so he can follow my footsteps. "Let's find the trail, Grandpa. Then we'll follow it to the shelter."

Our headlamps are bouncing light across the dark morning ground.

"You're going to love it here," he says. "It's the best place to raise a little girl."

He still doesn't understand that I'm me. I'm Robinson.

It scares me that he thinks I'm my pregnant mom, but I also want to know the ending. What happened after my mom came to Vermont to live with my grandpa? What happened when she had me? What went wrong?

"What happens?" I call back to him. "What happens when I'm born? What happens to Eddie?"

He stops and takes a deep breath and squints into the dark morning like he's looking for the answer. "I don't know," he says.

It's like an icicle in the gut because I think he really might not know. Maybe he stuffed it so deep that he actually forgot, and I'll just never find out. I'll never know what happened to my mom.

"I'm so glad you're here, Eddie," he says and starts walking again.

It feels like I'm hiking through the woods with a stranger, except I've lived with him my whole life.

I keep saying over and over in my head that I'm Robinson and he's my grandpa, Charlie, and we're escaping the Department for Children and Families and Grace and Harold and everyone else who thinks they know what's best for us. No one knows my grandpa like I do, and he can't live without his right hand.

I'm weaving through the sugar maples and trudging uphill, shining my headlamp on the snow, looking in the melting snow for the snowshoe tracks of the people who walk this stretch of the Appalachian Trail in the winter.

"Stop!" Grandpa yells and it echoes off the sky.

I whip around fast. "Shhhh!" I whisper. Even though I know Grace probably isn't even awake yet, I imagine her following our footsteps and tracking us down.

"Stop, stop, stop! Don't leave me!" he calls. And I don't know if he's talking to me or to Eddie or someone else his memory stirred up.

"Come on, Grandpa," I whisper. "It's OK. I'm not leaving you."

"Come back!" he shouts and he starts to cry and yell and I'm more scared than I've ever been because I want him to stop yelling and crying, but we can't go back. "Come back!" he sputters. I don't know why he's crying, if he just wants to go home or if he still thinks I'm Eddie and he's begging her to return, which is impossible because she's dead.

He falls to his knees. "Come back! Please! I'm sorry!"

"It's OK, Grandpa," I say. "I'm here. I'm not going

anywhere without you. Let's walk together." I reach out my hand and wait for him to catch up. Then we walk side by side, hand in hand, together up the hill until we reach the Appalachian Trail where Grandpa and I have hiked so many times. He's limping pretty badly on the right side and he keeps mumbling under his breath to please come back, please come back.

"We're close," I tell him and we continue on together up the trail, our things weighing heavy on my shoulders, but I know I can carry them all the way until the end.

We get to the sign that reads *.1 mile to shelter* and an arrow points down the trail.

"Almost there, Grandpa. Then we'll rest." *And the sun will rise up*, I'm thinking, *and you'll be good as new.*

There's no one in the shelter this time of year. All the hikers go through with their big beards and their big packs in the summer, so it's just Grandpa and me now.

"Here we are," I say and drop the pack on the wood floor of the shelter. In the summer, it's a good thing that the shelter has only three sides. This is where Grandpa and I stop to eat our lunch on warm afternoon hikes when school's out and where we dangle our feet from the edge of the shelter and take off our hiking boots and wiggle our toes. Plus, all the hikers who are going a long way with big packs smell like moose crap and I wouldn't want to be shut in anywhere with them. Today, though, I wish that there was a fourth wall, a front to the shelter so the wind wouldn't find its way inside to us.

I unpack my sleeping bag and the blanket from the couch. "Here, Grandpa, take this." I hand him my sleeping bag because it's warmer. "We'll just have a little breakfast and rest for a while. Then we'll go back home." I look at my watch. 7:04. If we can just wait until eight, then the coast will be clear until Grandpa and I can make a better plan.

Grandpa unties his boots and pulls his right foot into his lap. A big blister bubbles from the back of his heel, probably because he didn't tie his boots tight enough and it's hard walking in snow. I should have told him to lace them tighter, but I feel good that I at least remembered the first-aid kit because I can cut Grandpa a piece of Moleskin and wrap his heel with a Band-Aid and medical tape.

"That'll help," I say. He pulls his sock back on over his sore, wrapped blister.

Then he zips himself feet first into the sleeping bag and I wrap the blanket around my shoulders and huddle in close to him. The hair on his chin is rough and scratchy but feels good pressed up on my cheek.

We eat cheese sandwiches and drink water from the water bottle, and I'm thinking any minute now the sun will come up and Grandpa's memory will snap back to normal. But he's rubbing his head and mumbling.

"It's OK, Grandpa," I keep saying. "We'll go home soon."

Then he looks right at me, but I can tell it's not me he sees. "Eddie? Eddie. You can't leave us, Eddie," he says. Then he pushes the sleeping bag off his legs and stands up so fast that he wobbles on his socked feet. In one hand he grabs my pack and cradles it in the crook of his arm like it's a baby. With his other hand he grabs my arm hard. "Come on," he says. "I have to get you to the hospital. Wake up." And before I know it he's pushing me out of the shelter and into the woods.

"Grandpa, your boots!" He's sinking far into the snow in just his socks, and he's zipping the pack into his jacket like he's trying to keep a baby warm and pulling me along.

"We don't have time! We should have gone yesterday. Eddie, I'm sorry. I'm sorry." And he's crying again and pulling me deeper into the woods until I can't see the shelter anymore and we're not on the trail and I don't know if we're getting closer to home or farther.

Now I'm more scared than ever because I think we're lost and Grandpa's memory has never been so bad. He's not just misplacing his flannel or keys; he's misplacing his whole self, and I don't want to lose him. I want him to look right at me and say, *Robinson*. I want him to say he's cold and he needs his boots and that we should go home and what are we doing up here anyway? I want him to put his arm around me and say, *Everything is going to be OK, Robinson. Everything is going to be OK.*

But he's not. He's running wild like a spooked animal and pulling me hard through the woods.

"Hospital," he's panting. "Stay with me. I've got the baby."

I look at Grandpa cradling the pack as he runs, and he's looking down inside his jacket to check. And I know he sees me in there. He sees little baby me. And I wonder what happened to Eddie, what happened to my mom? Why was it too late? But I don't even care anymore. I'd rather have Grandpa back to normal than learn what happened. I want him to stop. He's hurting my arm and he's shaking and scared and his eyes look like he's in so much pain remembering.

We're walking in circles and we're walking fast and I'm crying now too and yelling, "Grandpa! Grandpa!" And I want it to be all over, so I pull back hard on my arm and we both topple into the snow and he clutches hard around the pack in his jacket, protecting it from the fall. And I yell, "It's me. It's Robinson! Eddie's dead!"

I unzip his jacket and pull out the pack and shake it in front of his face. "I'm grown-up, Grandpa. I'm grown-up and I'm fine and I'm right here."

He's crying big cries and I'm hugging him hard and there are cold tears on my cheeks that feel like they'll be frozen there forever. He's shaking from the cold and I know I did a bad job of taking care of Grandpa. I don't even know where we are anymore, and his socks are soaking wet from the snow.

"We have to go home," I say.

I pull him up from the snow and we walk hand in hand, following our footprints backward. Grandpa walks ahead through the thin cold branches, and they whip back fast to lash me on the face. Each cold branch on my cheek feels like a punishment for taking him out here. For making his memory worse.

I finally see the roof of the shelter and I point. "Over there, Grandpa," I say. We duck beneath branches and make our way back to where we started. I help him sit on the edge, and he pulls his boots over his wet socks. I roll up the sleeping bag and blanket and stuff them back in the pack and hoist it over my shoulders. Somehow it feels heavier than when we started.

The sun is beginning to shine down through the branches of the maple trees, and if we wait for one more hour we'll probably be safe from Grace and the

Department for Children and Families, but Grandpa is shaking from the feet up and I don't want him to be scared and wild anymore, so I say, "Let's go," and we follow the Appalachian Trail back down toward our house.

chapter 24

I squeeze Grandpa's hand hard as we step out of the woods and into our backyard. She Roll is parked in the driveway, and I can hear Harold banging on our front door and hollering, "Robbie? Charlie?"

We keep walking slowly, side to side, side to side, across the yard until we can see Harold and Paul on our front steps. Then Grandpa raises his hand above his head. "Here!" he calls. "We're here!"

He squeezes my hand back and says, "I'm sorry."

I'm squeezing as hard as my cold fingers can and even though I'm telling Grandpa that it'll be OK, I don't know that it will be.

Harold rushes toward us and takes Grandpa's arm. "Where were you? Are you OK?"

"Fine, fine," Grandpa mutters.

"Just out for a walk," I say.

Harold looks at me with eyes full of worry, but he doesn't ask any more questions.

"There you are," Paul says, patting my shoulder. He has May in that backward-book-bag carrier thing, and she's fast asleep on his chest. Together we help Grandpa up the front steps and inside.

Grandpa's shoulders are still shaking a little, like a chill got into his bones and he's trying to shoo it off.

Harold puts a kettle of water on to boil while I get Grandpa's boots off and unwrap the bandage over his blister.

"Does it hurt?" I ask.

He looks up and I don't know if he sees Eddie or me, but I can see him searching for his words.

"No," he says. Then he pats my shoulder. "No, Robbie."

And my eyes get all watery because I got my grandpa back.

Harold's pouring a kettle of boiling water into a basin in front of the couch, so I walk Grandpa over, help him sit down, and lift his feet into the hot water.

Harold sits down in our chair near him and rocks May as she gurgles awake. "How's that feel, Charlie? Temperature OK?"

"I'm fine, I'm fine," Grandpa grumbles. "I don't need all this fussing over. I'm not a hundred years old, you know." He shrugs off the blanket I put around his shoulders.

He's sounding more like the real Grandpa already.

Then I hear a car pull into the driveway and I know who it is and I'm not going to the door to welcome her in even though that's how Grandpa raised me. To be polite.

I take the kettle from Harold and go to the kitchen to fill it up and boil some more.

Harold greets Grace at the door and she says hi to my grandpa and Paul and goo-goo-gah-gahs over May. I can hear her unzip her jacket, and I'm thinking, *Keep it on because you're not staying long.*

Then before I know it she's in the kitchen standing next to me. "Your grandpa told me you are one remarkable girl," she says. "Now I really see what he's talking about." I turn on the faucet full blast because I want to drown her out.

Yeah, pretty remarkable, I'm thinking. *I woke him up in the middle of the night when I know his memory is most tired, I got him all confused and turned around, and I almost froze him to death out in the woods.*

The water starts overflowing from the kettle, so I turn off the faucet and put the kettle on the stove. The gas clicks as I start the burner and the flame jumps up.

"He means a lot to you," Grace says. "And I know you'd do anything for him. In fact, it seems like you have been doing quite a lot for him for a while."

I think about all the times I've put his flannel by the door so he wouldn't have to find it in the cupboard and get mad at himself, or how I sometimes turn the blinker on in the truck before the turns come up so he knows which way to go. I think about finding the ends of his sentences.

"You mean a lot to him too, you know," Grace says. "He loves you so much."

I stay facing the stove so I don't have to look at her. And I'm starting to think about Grandpa trying to get my mom to the hospital and how he held that bundle, me, so close to his heart in his jacket. And I'm thinking about all the lines on my stupid family tree that don't mean anything. Except Grandpa.

And before I know it I'm saying, "He's my only family," except I say it more to the kettle than to Grace.

"I know," she says, and puts her hand on my shoulder. The steam from the kettle is starting to whistle through the spout and it feels good on my face. "Why don't you bring that hot water to your grandpa," she says. "I bet he wants you to sit by him."

That's the truth. I'll sit right at his right hand.

I take the kettle into the living room and pour it into

the basin at Grandpa's feet. Then I sit down on the couch next to him and let him put his arm around me and I lean into that rough sandpaper on his chin.

Grace is opening a bag of piping hot fresh doughnuts. I take one and break it in half—one part for me, one for Grandpa.

Harold's sitting across from us with May in his lap, feeding her a bottle, and Paul is next to him and both their eyes look a little watery.

"Can you help me with a problem, Rob?" Harold asks. And it feels like we're back in the garage and he needs me to check under the hood of a sedan to make sure he's done everything right and didn't miss anything.

"Second opinion?" I ask.

He nods his head. Then he starts telling me that Grace and a nurse spent some time yesterday morning with Grandpa and there's something in his brain called Alzheimer's and that's what's making his memory so tired.

"It will get better if I act better," I tell them.

Grace says no, that's not how it works. That this has nothing to do with me. "It happens to some people when they get older. It's nobody's fault."

Just hearing that makes me feel like I dropped a heavy pack off my shoulders, and I take a big bite of the doughnut and it's as good as it smells.

"How can we fix it?" I ask Harold.

Grandpa sighs heavy, and I can feel his breath on my face. It smells like donuts and coffee.

"It's not going to get better," Harold says. "That's the hard part."

He reaches over and pats my knee, but I'm shaking my head and sitting up and looking right at Grandpa. "That's not true," I say. But Grandpa's eyes are getting watery like Harold's and I know that Grace is getting ready to take me away to a place for kids who have no family at all.

"We can't fix it, Robbie. No one can fix it," Harold says. "But we have a plan, and we need your second opinion." He puts down May's bottle and rocks her in his arms.

The whole room looks like it's underwater.

"You and your grandpa are doing great here together right now," he says. "But there are some times when he needs a little more help, like at night, when he's more forgetful. We were thinking of having a really nice nurse come to help you guys in the evenings with dinner and getting ready for bed."

I want to say no way, that I can make dinner and help Grandpa just fine. But I remember Ms. Gloria and think about Harold's plan for a full count to ten. And each count I feel more OK.

"And you'll keep an eye on him at the garage?" I ask. "Just in case?"

"Of course."

My eyes are burning, but I'm still listening.

"Then when Charlie's memory gets too bad and it's too hard for him to be here at home, he told us he wants to go live somewhere that will help him full-time," Harold says.

"What? Grandpa, where?"

Grandpa squeezes my shoulder and says. "Just a place for old guys like me up the road," he says. "It's nice there and you can visible . . ." He shakes his head. "Visible me."

And I know he means I can visit him. "Every day?" I ask.

Grandpa nods his head yes.

"What's it called?" I ask.

Grandpa opens his mouth but shakes his head and looks up to the ceiling like he's searching for the name up there.

"Mountain View," Grace says. "It's only a ten-minute drive from here."

"But what about me? When he goes to . . . where will I . . . ? I can't go with him?"

"Robbie." Something catches in Harold's voice and he wipes his eyes with his shirtsleeve over sleeping May's little face, and Paul reaches out and grabs his hand. They hold hands tight, fingers all interlaced like the braids Grandpa makes.

"Robbie," Harold says, and he waits until I'm looking right at him before he starts talking again, but his eyes look all watery and I'm shaking even though I'm not cold. "Paul and I were hoping you'd come live with us when your grandpa decides to go to Mountain View."

"We love you so much," Paul says. "And we already think of you as family."

I'm shivering hard and the tears trapped in my eyes are running now. I can feel them dropping off my chin.

"And we'll be visiting your grandpa every day anyway," Harold says. "And May would be lucky to have you as a big sister."

My voice is shaking, but before I know it I'm saying yes. Yes to visiting Grandpa every day and yes to living with Harold and Paul and being May's big sister and yes to continuing working on cars in the garage and teaching Harold how to boil sap so we can bring some syrup to Grandpa in case they only have the fake stuff at Mountain View.

"Whenever you two are ready," Harold says to Grandpa and me. "We're here."

Grace is nodding, and even her eyes are a little

watery and I'm starting to think she isn't half as bad as I thought before.

Harold holds out his fist to me and I bump it with mine. "Deal," I say.

Grandpa's kissing my face and telling me that we'll never really be apart and that there's no chance he'll ever forget me, even if it seems like it sometimes.

"You live here in me," he says and taps his thumb at his heart. "Not here," he says, pointing at his head. Then he brings his hand back down and rests it on his chest. "And I'll never lose this."

I lean back into his sandpaper chin and Harold comes across and sits next to us and Paul does too and May's reaching out for my finger and I let her, and before I know it I'm smushed between them and it feels pretty OK. Really OK.

chapter 25

It's easy to talk Grandpa and Harold and Paul into letting me take the day off from school. They're all feeling
pretty mushy, so mushy that I bet they'd buy me my own
Toyota Tacoma if I asked them nice.

"As long as you do your homework," Harold says.
And he's doing that practice dad thing again, which isn't
so annoying anymore because I know he's just practicing
for me.

I walk Grace and Harold and Paul out to their cars,
and Grace tells me that a nurse will come by at five
thirty every night, starting tonight. "Her name is Katie
and she's the best."

She tells me how Katie will help Grandpa transi-
tion from afternoon to evening and into bed at night,

and how she'll make sure he has clean clothes, and help with dinner. I tell her that's fine, but really I'm thinking that I'm still going to squeeze the cheese into the mac no matter what because that's my job. And that Grandpa can still braid my hair in the morning.

Harold gives me a hug good-bye while Paul puts May in her car seat and says to call if I need anything.

Back in the house I help Grandpa empty the water from the basin at his feet. It's not hot anymore, but that's fine because we're not shaking like we were before.

"My memory might be rusty," he says, "but that doesn't mean I forgot about that homework you have to do. You're not getting any free day out of me."

I remember the pact I made with Alex. That even though it stinks and we don't want to do it we are going to finish this stupid family tree project so we can pass the fifth grade. And so he can make his dad proud. And it's due tomorrow.

"Will you help me?" I ask.

Grandpa nods so I go to my book bag and take out my notebook and a pen and drop it on the kitchen table. He walks over slow and pulls out a chair to sit.

My stomach is growling. That cheese sandwich we had in the shelter already feels like days ago. Even the doughnut from Grace feels like yesterday. "I'm going to make some oatmeal," I tell Grandpa.

"Make it two," he says.

I stir in the oats and turn down the heat so it doesn't boil over, then I grab two bowls and spoons from the cabinet.

"Don't forget the syrup."

I smile at him because we both know that no one worth knowing can eat oatmeal without maple syrup. But when I go to pour it over the oats in our bowls, the slowest, skinniest stream dribbles out.

"Guess we'll have to boil soon, then," Grandpa says. "A refrigerator without syrup is no good at all."

And I don't know if he remembers when Derek and his mom came over, and if he remembers about his hands and spilling half the sap.

"How about this weekend?" he asks.

"Perfect." I'm already thinking that I'll go out today after I finish this stupid project to collect sap from the buckets and get ready.

I let the last drops fall from the maple syrup jug and bring the bowls of oatmeal over to the kitchen table, where Grandpa is sitting with my unfinished family tree draft.

And that's when I get the idea for my project.

chapter 26

I'm sticking my work gloves into the cracks of the sugar maple tree and pulling off pieces of bark and snapping twigs from the branches and collecting it all in an extra sap bucket.

"I don't have any poster board or anything to put it on," I say.

Grandpa starts walking to the shed and waves me along. "Let's see if we can't find something in here."

Our shed is a mess. Grandpa's workbench is covered with tools and old car parts and bottles of oil. Spare tires are stacked in the corner, and my baseball bats are sticking up out of them.

Grandpa's digging through an old metal shelf and I'm thinking there's no way he's going to find anything in this place when he holds up an old green Vermont license plate like the ones on our truck. "How about this?"

I'm thinking he must have forgotten what he was looking for, because how can I use a license plate as poster board for my family tree? But then he says, "We'll need some Gorilla Glue too," and starts digging through his toolbox. "Aha! Here it is."

We bring everything back inside and lay it all out on the kitchen table. "Let's make that tree," Grandpa says.

So I turn the license plate the tall way and start laying the bark out on it for the trunk and then add the twigs for the branches. They stick out off the sides of the license plate.

It doesn't look like a perfect sugar maple or anything, but it's way better than the stupid lines in my notebook. Grandpa's turning over the bark, squeezing Gorilla Glue, then I press the bark hard into the license plate and Grandpa presses his hands down on mine to make the glue stick. "This should strike . . ." he says, but he shakes his head and presses harder down on my hands.

And it does. It does stick just fine. So we glue each piece and all the twigs pressing hand over hand over hand over hand until there's a miniature sugar maple glued on the old Vermont license plate. And even though this project is stupid and I don't like artsy things that much at all, it looks pretty OK since I like cars and maple trees.

"Look at that, Robbie!" Grandpa admires, pointing at the project.

But I know it's not done. I still have the hard part left to do. I still have to put on the names.

I push my notebook toward him and say, "This is what I have so far."

Grandpa looks at my draft and runs his finger over Eddie's name. And then over Lucy's name. Then he laughs at "mean old lady" and "mean old man."

"They *were* kind of mean," he chuckles. "But Lucy. Lucy was a gem. Just not so strong as Eddie and you." But then he gets all quiet again just when I was thinking he was going to tell me more. But he closes up tight instead, and I can tell he's not going to say any more than that.

"Forget it," I say. "I don't want to put any of them on my tree because I don't know a thing about them." Heat rises up to my face. "I can't just hand in a stupid piece of bark." I push my notebook clear off the kitchen table.

"Robbie," he says.

And even though I feel bad that I trudged him through the stupid snow this morning, I'm mad he won't actually help me with my family tree. So I say forget it,

I'm going outside to collect the sap from the buckets and I don't need his help.

"Robbie—" he says.

"Forget it, Grandpa!" I yell. "Forget it. Just keep everything inside and to yourself until you don't remember anything anymore." And what I'm thinking is that Grandpa needs Group Guidance with Ms. Gloria to teach him how to tap deep through his hard bark and open up.

The door slams behind me and the cold air feels good. I take my time emptying the buckets and packing the snow back up around the plastic collection jugs, but I can't stay out very long because I rushed out mad without my jacket and I'm starting to shiver again like this morning.

When I go back inside, Grandpa's coming down the stairs. "Sit," he says and points to the kitchen table.

"I'm not doing the proj—"

"I said sit."

I slump hard in the chair, but I grab my Dodgers hat out of my book bag and pull it down over my face.

Grandpa sits down too and before I know it he's sliding a picture across the table. I can't see anything past the brim of my hat, just this picture of a woman with a boy-short haircut, skin the color of sugar maple bark, and a big pregnant belly. In the picture my grandpa's got his arm around her and he's smiling big. He looks a lot younger and like he's not confused about anything at all. Like he knows exactly where his flannel is and where the bathroom is when he gets up in the middle of the night to use it.

Then Grandpa taps his finger on the woman. "That's your mom," he tells me. "That's Eddie."

"Where were you keeping this? Why didn't you ever show—"

"It's here now."

I don't want to be mad at Grandpa, but I am. He had a picture this whole time and who knows if he has any more and who knows all the things about my mom he's keeping from me?

And I think of Ms. Gloria telling me to use the family tree project to help me talk to Grandpa. It hasn't worked that well so far, but it has to work today. It has to work today because I can't wait anymore and I don't know when Grandpa will go live with the old people at Mountain View, and because my family tree is due tomorrow.

"I need to know more for this project," I say. He nods. "When we were in the woods this morning, you kept calling me Eddie," I remind him. "You said you had to get to the hospital."

I look up at him from under the brim of my hat.

"I did?" he asks. "I don't remember—I'm sorry."

"Don't be sorry, Grandpa. It was the most you ever

told me about her." I look down at the picture on the table and turn my hat around backward so he can look right at me. "What happened?" I ask. "Tell me before you forget."

Grandpa takes a deep breath and slides the picture back in front of him. "I don't think I'll ever forget. She lives here too," he says and taps his chest. "Right next to you."

I pat his hand and say that it's OK, he can tell me. He holds the picture between his thumb and forefinger and it shakes a little as he looks.

"She came to Vermont to give birth and raise you here," he starts. "Her mom, Lucy, had passed away from a heart attack. Eddie wanted you to have a relationship with me, a relationship that she didn't really get since Lucy and I never lived together after she found out she was pregnant with your mom."

He puts the picture down and traces her belly with his finger. "I loved her so much," he says. "I made her healthy food for the baby and built her a crib out in the shed from real Vermont wood."

I pictured Grandpa sanding the wood in the shed and hammering the pieces together tight.

He's still looking down at the picture. "It was a hard labor, but she was the happiest in her whole life when you were born. She hadn't named you yet when we brought you home. We called you 'little fighter' because . . ."

Grandpa is losing his words, but I don't know the end to this sentence, so he needs to finish it.

"Why'd you call me 'little fighter'?" I ask.

He nods and taps his finger on the table. "Little fighter . . . because you were small," he continues, "and strong and you balled your fists up tight and made your voice heard all through the night right from the beginning."

I try to picture my mom walking around our house with me in her arms as I cried out at the top of my lungs, and even imagining it makes me feel good.

"Your second and third day home from the hospital she ran a fever. Sweated through her sheets. The doctors had said it might take a few weeks for your mom to feel strong again, so I didn't worry. I thought if the fever didn't go down after another night I'd take her in to get checked the next morning."

Then this morning in the woods all makes sense. Grandpa shoving the pack deep in his coat like it was a little fighter baby he was trying to keep warm, and pulling me through the woods telling Eddie to hold on, not to leave him. He was reliving that moment, trying to get my mom back to the hospital in time.

"The next day she was way worse, wasn't she, Grandpa?" I pat his hand and take the picture from him.

"It was too late," he says. "An infection had dug too deep. And I didn't even . . ."

Grandpa puts his head in his hands and his shoulders are shaking and I know how he feels. Like it's his fault.

"It's no one's fault," I tell him, and for the first time I believe that. It's not my fault my mom died, and it's not his either. It's just plain old unfair bad luck, like Alex's dad and Ms. Gloria's son. Grandpa grabs my hand and squeezes it hard.

"What happened after she died?" I asked.

Grandpa's looking up at the ceiling like he's remembering. "We buried her in a field of sunflowers in New Hampshire. Next to her mom. Next to Lucy."

"I was there?"

Grandpa nods. "I held you the whole time. You balled your fists and cried. Then I brought you home and gave you the strongest fighter name I knew."

"Robinson Hart," I say.

"Robinson Hart."

I'm thinking about the big question mark I have on my family tree. "Did she ever talk about my dad?"

"Your dad?" Grandpa repeats. "Eddie never once talked about your dad, and I just let her be on that." Then he kind of smiles a little while he's remembering. "Eddie wanted a child more than anything." He smiles a little more and I can picture my mom with her big smile and sticking-up boy-cut hair. "You were all Eddie's," he says.

I laugh with him a little because it feels good to laugh. "Now I'm all yours," I say, and he taps his big finger on his heart.

"All mine."

Then I pick up my notebook from the floor and slide over the maple tree license plate. "I think I'm ready to finish the project."

chapter 27

"Your project is so cool!" Derek shouts as if I'm not sitting right next to him, and I don't try to shut him up or anything even though other kids are starting to look over.

I shrug my shoulders like it's no big deal, but I'm kind of happy he's looking at it so close.

"You put me on there?" he says as soon as he sees his name dangling from one of the maple branches. Then he full-on hugs me even though he knows I don't do hugs or anything like that. I don't hug him back, but I don't shove him off either.

He's touching the bark of the sugar maple and running his fingers in the grooves of the Vermont license plate. "It's perfect," he says.

Then he slides his project over to me. His board game idea came out cool too, with a stack of cards in the middle just like a real board game. "Pick the top card," he tells me.

I turn over the top card and there's a picture of him and me holding a big jug of syrup from boiling last year. He's lifting up the jug to his mouth, pretending to chug it, and I'm rolling my eyes. Under the picture it says *Robinson Hart. Best friend I'll ever have.*

I nudge his shoe with my shoe under the table and say thanks. "That reminds me," I tell him. "We're going to try boiling again this weekend. Tell your mom."

"Maple Day! Wouldn't miss it." He nudges my shoe back with his.

Ms. Meg is telling everyone to take out their projects. She says we're going to spend the next couple of periods practicing presenting before our families come this afternoon for the open house. I'm thinking that I don't need to practice because Grandpa will be working at the garage. And I already know he likes my project. And I don't really care what any other parents think.

Candace sits down at the table with us. "Let me see!" She slides my project over to her. And before I know it Alex is huddling around and Oscar is too.

"It looks so cool!" Oscar says. He touches all the names that dangle down from twine off the twigs.

Oscar's is really good too. The sketch of himself between the two trees looks just like him. One tree is for his mom's side of the family and the other is for his dad's. I remember everything he was saying in Group Guidance and I know why he made his project like that. He feels like he's in the middle of his parents splitting up.

Candace finished hers too. I tell her I like how all the happy pictures of Tessa and her are right in the middle of her tree.

Oscar says, "I bet you'll have lots more happy pictures with her too. It'll all work out."

Candace nods and smiles and says she knows.

I turn to Alex. "We had a pact," I remind him.

He unzips his book bag and pulls out a piece of folded white notebook paper. It's small and sketched in black ink. "It's not that good, but I don't care," he says. "At least it's done."

It's a simple drawing of a tree, but you can see the roots digging down below the ground. That's where he labeled his dad.

"It's really good," I tell him and I reach out like Harold does to me sometimes and give him a fist bump.

"I made my Grandpa the trunk of my tree," I say. "But he's kind of like my roots too, I guess."

And it feels pretty OK having everyone look at my family tree project because it's not so bad.

Even Ms. Gloria and Mr. Danny come to the classroom to see our projects and Ms. Gloria puts her arm around my shoulders when she looks at the names dangling from the sugar maple twigs and sees hers. Her windshield-washer-blue eyes get all teary and she says she's really proud of me.

I tell her something that Grandpa told me last night, which is how I figured out how to finish my project. He said that you should hold close the people who push you to be the best version of yourself. "That's what family does," Grandpa said. "They push you to be your best and love you no matter what."

That sounds like Ms. Gloria to me, and everyone else I put on there, except maybe May because she's just a baby. But I guess it's my job to help her be her best version and love her no matter what. And that makes her family too.

Before I know it Ms. Meg and Ms. Gloria are handing out after-school snacks and lining us all up to use the bathroom because parents are starting to come.

Our job is to say "Welcome to our classroom" to all the parents who show up, but I just look down at my Nike Air Griffeys and let Candace talk to the adults.

All the parents are sitting down at our tables and it looks funny to see them in our classroom. Then Candace pokes me and points. "My sister came!" she whispers. "I put the invitation on her bed last night, but I didn't think she'd actually be here." Her sister is sitting in the front row with a purple streak dyed through her hair, and she smiles big when Candace spots her. Then I see her mouth, *Good luck*.

I give Candace a secret thumbs-up.

Ms. Meg is in the front of the room welcoming the parents and telling them how hard we worked on these projects.

"Now it's time to hear a short explanation from the students about the choices they made on their family trees," Ms. Meg announces.

Brittany is the first to go. Then Chelsea. They pretty much have the same papier-mâché tree project, and they talk about how fun it was to paint it once it hardened. Then Ronald goes. He talks about how his brother is really important to him, so he put him at the top of his project. Then Derek presents his board game and his mom cheers from the front row. Alex shares next, and he's looking right at me the whole time he's talking about his tree drawing. He points to the roots that dig deep below the soil. His mom and brothers aren't here, and I don't want to think of what they're doing, so I just look right back at him because I think it's making us both feel OK.

"Robinson?" Ms. Meg says. "Your turn."

My stomach feels like two outs bottom of the ninth, but I stand up and walk to the front of my room and all of a sudden I'm thinking that maybe my license plate tree is stupid and I don't have anything to say about it.

"This is mine," I say and hold it up. I catch Ms. Gloria's eye, which is enough to remind me to turn my hat around backward.

Then before I know it the classroom door is creaking open and my grandpa pokes his head in. "Found it," he says and Ms. Gloria waves him in and helps him to a seat. Behind him are Harold and Paul, and May is wrapped up and sleeping in Harold's arms. Katie, Grandpa's nurse, is here even though it's way earlier than five thirty, and that's when she's supposed to start helping us. I've only known her one day, but she doesn't seem half-bad because she doesn't have to be here and she is and she didn't make my grandpa feel stupid when she was helping him last night, even with the simple things, and she let me squeeze the cheese into the mac. She smiles big and pats my grandpa's arm. Harold gives me an air fist bump over sleeping May.

I point to the trunk of my tree and say, "My Grandpa is my trunk. He's the one who takes care of me." Then I point to Eddie's branch. "My mom was just like me. A fighter with a boy name." Then I point to the other branches. "These people aren't actually related to me, but they're still family. Ms. Gloria. Derek. Harold and Paul and May." I don't really have anything else to say, but it feels like everyone else talked way longer about their projects. Everyone's watching me, expecting more, and it makes me feel weird. I'm looking at Grandpa's nurse Katie and thinking that maybe I should have put her on the tree because she isn't so bad and she's going to be around for a while and she came all the way to school to see my project.

Then I decide I could always add people as I go.

I look at Harold again and I remember how I want to represent my family well, so I try to think about something else I can say.

"I guess family is something you get like I got my Grandpa, but it's also something you make." And I'm looking at Derek, who's nodding his head and giving me a thumbs-up, and then at Grandpa, whose eyes are all misty and proud. Then Grandpa stands up and claps and everyone else claps too and it feels just like sliding into home.

chapter 28

"Maple Day!" Derek's yelling out the window of their Subaru Outback before they even pull into our driveway Saturday morning. "Maple Daaaaaaaaaay!"

The fire's burning hot already, and I'm showing Harold how we put the metal bars over the brick fire pit and fill the lobster pot with sap. I'm telling him how we wait for it to boil down before we can filter it into our empty maple syrup jugs we have stacked high in the shed. I can tell he's paying attention too, because he's nodding at each step.

"While we're waiting for it to boil down, is anyone hungry?" Harold asks. "I can take a quick trip to Dean and Walt's and bring back some burgers."

"Wait! I know!" I say, and I run big strides back to

the house and track slush and mud right through the living room and kitchen to the refrigerator because I'm so excited to show Harold how we boil eggs on Maple Day.

"Can we?" I ask Grandpa when I get back outside, showing him the half-dozen egg carton I took from the refrigerator.

He nods, and Derek and I each drop three eggs carefully in the boiling sap. "Seven minutes," I say.

"Brilliant," Harold says. Then he's asking me questions about Grade A Golden versus Amber and Dark, and I'm explaining about the time of year and how we'll probably get Grade A Dark syrup this time because it's late enough in the season that the snow is starting to melt and it'll really feel like spring soon.

Then I don't even know why, but I start thinking about Alex and whether his dad will be alive when the snow melts and it's the saddest thought, so I try to wipe it out of my head but I can't.

Grandpa uses the ladle to scoop the eggs out of the sap and drops them in the snow to cool the shells before he peels them.

The eggs are perfect. I love when they come out not too hard-boiled so the yolks are still a little soft and they have the slightest maple taste and they're still warm from the pot.

"Heaven," Harold sputters, his mouth full of egg.

I'm glad Harold is learning about how to stoke the fire and boil the sap down and filter the syrup and seal it into jugs. I'm a good teacher and I know it better than anybody because Grandpa taught me.

When the syrup is ready I take the first ladle of it and pour it on the clean snow near the sugar maple trees where there are new buds popping up through the snow. Derek goes headfirst right into it. "Yum!" he exclaims, but his mouth is so full of snow and sugar that you can hardly understand him.

I scoop mine into a loose snowball and eat it out of my hands. The cold snow stings my teeth, but the maple is sweet and perfect and makes the sting go away.

Harold and Grandpa and Derek's mom scoop some up too. And before we know it we're laughing and pouring out more maple for sugar on snow. And I remember when we were all laughing with Ms. Gloria in Group Guidance and how good it felt and I'm thinking that maybe when we boil next year I'll invite Candace and Oscar and maybe even Alex. Little May will be walking and she'll have her first sugar on snow and Grandpa will be here to see the new buds popping up through the snow by the maple trees.

Grandpa puts his hand on my shoulder. "Time to pull out the taps, I'd say." He points to the metal taps we hammered into the trees at the beginning of the season.

"I got it."

As I'm pulling and wiggling the taps out of the trunks, I'm thinking about what Grandpa always says. Everything, even a tree, has sweetness at its core. And I'm thinking maybe that is true, even if it's under a layer of tough bark and all mixed up with splinters and knots.

acknowledgments

Thank you first to my mom and dad. You got me a card to the Shelburne Library before I could even read, and then understood when I wanted to own all the books I loved anyway. I learned, in your laps, that books are comfort and adventure, and would have a forever-place in my life.

And to my big brother, Tyler—you told me that Robinson was worthy and she needed to be sent out in the world. All my life I've been looking up to you and listening very carefully to what you say, and I'm so thankful you said this.

I'm very lucky to be surrounded by great readers who took the time to live in Robbie's world with me as I was creating it. Jess Rothenberg, Jennifer Ochoa, Stephanie

Douglas, Gina Salerno, and Janine Stellacci, thank you for reading, listening, and encouraging.

I'm forever grateful for the Vermont College of Fine Arts community and the magic that exists up on that hill in Montpelier. In particular, thank you to my advisors, Alan Cumyn, Tim Wynne-Jones, Coe Booth, and Shelley Tanaka. I still hear your wise voices in my head while I'm writing.

Thank you to all the students and faculty of MS 324 in New York City. It was in that building, those classrooms, with you, that I realized I must write.

And thank you to the teachers I have had along the way for encouraging creativity and kindness. You may notice bits of yourselves in Robinson's story.

I have the most incredible support and excitement from my agent, Stephen Barbara; editor, Erica Sussman; and the many people at HarperCollins who had a hand in *Just Like Jackie*. Thank you again and again for your vision, your collaboration, and your guidance. You are my dream team.

And to my husband, Kamahnie, and son, Miles—you inspire and motivate me every day. I am most proud that I'm on your tree.

Don't miss Lindsey Stoddard's next book!

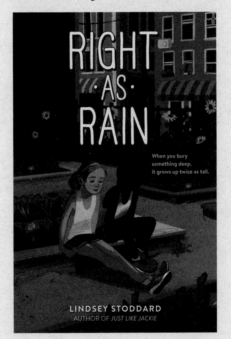

CHAPTER 1

Dirt

The earliest thing I can remember is dirt jammed beneath my fingernails.

My mom studies the brain, so I know about childhood amnesia. It means we can't remember anything before the age of three or four. That's a fact because when I close my eyes and play memory games—Mom gives me a word and I try to connect it to moments I remember as far back as I can go—the earliest I can ever come up with is the dirt. Everything before that, before I was three, is just a big who-knows.

The dirt jammed under my fingernails when I was three felt good, though. Like it was supposed to be there and I wasn't my whole full self without it.

My mom says that memories stick best when we tell

them into stories with feelings and smells and colors. Maybe that's why I remember the dirt so well, because it felt so good, and because my family has been telling that story my whole life, so I know all the details even if I didn't recall them on my own.

Here's how it goes:

I'd wait until my mom and dad weren't looking. Then my little fingers would get to work on the line of buttons or long zipper that started at the back of my neck, whatever dress my mom stuck me in that day. She thought a dress made out of denim or corduroy was a compromise, but a dress is a dress, and I wouldn't be caught dead in one. I only ever wanted my brother's hand-me-downs, knee-ripped overalls and flannel shirts.

Once I got free of the zipper or buttons or stretched the fabric off over my head, I'd make a break for it and run my three-year-old, bare-naked butt to my dad's garden in the backyard and I'd bury it. I'd bury my dress as deep as I could, in with the downward-growing carrots and among the potatoes bigger than my little-kid fists.

Then I felt free. I felt just right with the dress deep in the earth, my baby skin open to the summer sun, and the Vermont soil packed under my nails.

It would only last a few minutes before my mom would find me in the yard and ask, "Rain, where is your dress?" I'd shrug and say that's a big who-knows, and that maybe it ran off to be with a little girl who would love it more than I did.

Until one day when I made my naked break to the garden with a patchwork dress bunched up in my right fist, and stopped dead in my tracks. There were dresses everywhere. Every dress I had ever buried and more. Pink lace, yellow cotton, long denim with buttons, corduroy with big front pockets, white tulle, and navy striped ruffles hanging from the tomato plants and strewn across the thick-growing kale.

Then I felt my mom's hand on my head. "Remember, Rain, when you bury things deep, they grow up twice as tall."

I remember the screen door slam and my dad walking out to the garden. He draped his arm around my mom's shoulders. "Look what sprouted up," he said, and they both tried to hide little laughs behind their hands.

The screen door slammed again and Guthrie rushed out to the yard and snapped a picture that lives in one of our family albums—his naked baby sister wide-eyed and jaw-dropped among the colorful gowns budding up. He laughed too and patted my head, but the idea of a dress garden made me cry big tears, so they bit their tongues and helped me harvest all the frill and lace in the dirty wicker basket that usually carried leaves of red lettuce and sun-warmed tomatoes.

That day, with my nails still full of dirt, I swore to myself that I'd never bury anything that deep again.

But that was before I was ten years old, when my parents laughed and talked to each other in normal tones. When we were a family of four.

Before that night.

CHAPTER 2

That Night

"Promise you won't tell," he said.

"Promise." I stuck out my hand and we locked our pinkies in a pact.

CHAPTER 3

Moving

"That's it?" I ask. "It's technically not even a truck. It's a van." That's a fact, because vans have those sliding doors on the sides and so does the vehicle parked in our driveway.

"Yes, Rain." My mom's pulling clear tape across a box marked *Towels*. "That's it, for the hundredth time."

I've actually only asked three times, but each time I can't believe it. We're moving 288 miles to New York City, and everything we're taking with us can fit through the sliding doors of that van.

"That's what selling the house furnished means. We leave the furniture."

I want to tell her that I might have agreed to moving, but I never agreed to leaving all my stuff. Especially my bed. I like my bed because it has two inches of foam on top that remembers the shape of my body no matter what position I sleep in.

And then there's my last memory of him, kneeling down and shaking me awake, whispering.

Hey, sleepyhead.

Locking pinkies.

Maybe it won't be so bad to leave the bed behind.

My mom presses the tape down over the edge of the box and rips it off the roll with her teeth. "This way we'll start fresh," she says. "We'll just get what we need when we get there." She tries to smooth the wrinkles out of the tape, but there's one right down the middle that sticks up and won't go away.

Instead of telling her that maybe I want my dresser or my desk or something from Guthrie's room, I try to think of what Dr. Cyn says about fresh starts.

Then my mom pops up from the box. "I have to go grab the . . ." But I can't hear what she's going to grab because she's already hustling up the stairs to their bedroom. She's always hustling off somewhere. Up the stairs, out to work, over to the grocery store. All the way to New York City.

I want to yell at her. Yell that she can get a new bed, a new apartment, and a new brain research job at Columbia Presbyterian Hospital in New York City, but that I don't want new friends, new teachers, and a new track coach when we're so close to the end of the school year. Especially this year.

But every time I really want to yell, I remember that when she sat me down forty-five days ago and asked about moving before the year was out, I nodded and said OK. I said OK because they need someone at the hospital by June first for a team-building week before a big conference, and people who study the brain know that building a team is important. I said OK because even though I've never met Dr. Cyn, I've been following her blog on families and grief for 278 days, and she says fresh starts can help a grieving family cope.

And I said OK because I remember what I did, and how nobody knows, and how if I hadn't done it, everything would be normal and no one would want to hustle off anywhere or stayed locked in a bedroom all day.

So instead of shouting at the back of my mom's head as she hustles up the stairs, I crack my knuckles and count the boxes stacked by the front door. *Towels. Books. Clothes—Maggie. Clothes—Henry. Clothes—Rain. Kitchen. School supplies—Rain. Garden.* There are thirteen in all, which feels unlucky.

I'm surprised to see the *Garden* box. Dad wants to leave his gardening stuff here, and Mom thinks he's just being difficult. I know because I heard them arguing about it when they first sold the house and were starting to pack. I was supposed to be shoveling the front walk. I'd already packed my big winter jacket, not thinking we'd get another storm because it was April. So instead of shoveling I was crouched in the back of my closet looking for an extra sweatshirt in my *Donations* box. Their bedroom is right on the other side of my closet wall, and I could hear every word.

Of course you're bringing it, Henry. You're not staying in the bedroom all day when we get there. You're acting like your life is over.

You're acting like yours isn't.

Don't.

Everything stays in this house. Isn't that your plan? So I'll leave it here, with all the other important stuff you're so ready to leave behind.

Henry—

Nothing to grow in New York City anyway.

Then the door slammed and I could hear my mom's feet hustling off somewhere. My dad didn't even call, *Maggie!* like he used to. Instead, I heard him slump on the bed and click off the light, even though it was only four o'clock in the afternoon.

I wanted to go crawl in with him, pull the comforter over our heads, and close my eyes tight against the slivers of late-afternoon light sneaking in through the blinds, and just let our hearts hurt. But the front walk needed to be shoveled, so I pulled on an old sweatshirt that would belong to some other kid by next month, and opened the door to the cold outside.

When I was shoveling the walk that afternoon I counted each pile of snow I dug out and tossed over my shoulder. My brain kept telling me if I could just get to thirty, then everything would go back to normal. I breathed in with each thrust, and out with each toss. The snow was wet and heavy because it was spring and too warm for the fluffy, pretty stuff. It felt good. It burned in my back and my shoulders, and I just kept counting. *Sixteen, seventeen, eighteen . . .*

After thirty, I dropped the shovel, fell back into the big pile I'd made, and looked up at the darkening sky. I knew nothing had actually changed, because shoveling thirty shovels never brought anyone back from the dead. And that's a fact.

Dad will come downstairs eventually, probably with his hair sticking up, and probably right before it's time to carry the boxes outside and get in the van and drive away. He'll see the box with *Garden* written in Mom's handwriting and they'll start up that stupid fight about whether it should stay or go.

Mom's feet are hustling back down the stairs. "OK,

I got them," she says, clutching a stack of three family photo albums. We used to keep them on the coffee table in the TV room and I'd look through them when the commercials were boring.

But after that night, they disappeared up behind the closed door of my parents' bedroom.

"I think they'll fit in here," she says, peeling the tape back off the *Towels* box and burying the albums down into the yellow terry cloth. My naked-butt-dress-garden photo is in the one on top. Then she pulls the tape back down across the box, but it doesn't stick as well and she still can't smooth out that wrinkle.

I wonder where she'll put the albums when we get to our new apartment.

"I'll start loading," I say, and grab the *Garden* box. I push my feet into my Converse and head down the front walk to the moving van. The box isn't heavy. Seedlings mostly, I bet, and from the sound of it, a couple of clinking trowels, and maybe a few pots. But there's no way to move the whole shed, the whole garden, the whole backyard where Dad taught Guthrie and me to measure, and till, and plant, and water.

I slide open the van door and put the box inside with mom's handwriting, *Garden*, hidden against the back of the driver's seat so Dad won't see.

Mom is walking down the path with two boxes labeled

Books stacked in her arms. "Keep that door open," she calls. "And go tell your dad we're packing the truck."

"Van," I say. "It's only a van." And before I yell something that I don't deserve to yell, I turn fast and crack my knuckles back up the path.

Their bedroom door is closed like it has been for the last 350 days. I knock as quietly as I can and put my ear to the door. "Dad?" I whisper.

I hear the comforter crinkle and my dad clear his throat. "Coming."

I back up on my tiptoes even though I know he's awake and I can't possibly ruin anything else by walking normally, or even stomping my feet hard on our wood floors like I really want to, but walking silently seems safer, just in case.

Guthrie's door has been closed for the last 350 days too. Or at least my mom thinks so. I've snuck in there exactly six times since that night just to lie on his floor in my sleeping bag, like I used to every Christmas Eve for as long as I can remember. When I was little we stayed up and made plans to catch Santa, even though now I know he hadn't believed in Santa for a long time, and was just playing along for me.

Each of those six times since that night, I've woken early, rolled up my sleeping bag, scuffed up his shag rug to hide the memory of my body, and snuck out before my mom could find me there. Even though I hate that she shut up his bedroom, I don't want to upset her any more by opening a door that she wants closed.

Now that I'm walking by his room, it feels like I should go in one last time before we leave forever. I know everything will be the same on the other side, but seven times seems lucky. So I turn his doorknob quietly and push it open.

It's exactly the same. His quilt is pulled back, and both pillows are still on the floor, where Mom threw them that night when she found them bunched under his sheets pretending to be his sleeping body. His English 12 textbook is open to page 194, and his coffee mug is still half-full and on his desk, like he's just in the bathroom and will be back any minute to slurp a sip and finish reading "A Sound of Thunder" by Ray Bradbury.

It's weird that Mom hasn't come in to make his bed and throw his textbook in the donation box, or return it to the school, or rinse his coffee mug and put it back in our fully furnished kitchen for the next teenage son who lives here to make his coffee black and walk upstairs to his room to read his English homework. She cleaned every other inch of the house, but she closed this door that night, and just hustles past it on her way to somewhere else.

"Rain! Henry! Are you coming?" Mom's voice breaks the silence of Guthrie's room.

"Coming!" I call. And without even thinking I reach into the guitar case that's lying open on the floor and grab one of Guthrie's guitar picks. I press the triangle of plastic between my fingers and imagine his fingers there. Then I stuff it in my jeans pocket.

I pull his door closed just as Dad opens their bedroom door and steps out. "Hey," he says. His voice sounds like it hasn't been used in days. His hair is sticking up on one side, his beard is grayer and scruffier and longer than I've ever seen it, and his flannel shirt is off by a button.

"Hey," I whisper back.

Then I'm the one hustling off and down the stairs.

Books by
LINDSEY STODDARD

HARPER
An Imprint of HarperCollinsPublishers

www.harpercollinschildrens.com